FINDING BUTTERCUP

FINDING BUTTERCUP

THERESA JANE

Printed in the United States of America

First Printing, 2017

ISBN-13: 978-1-945949-61-6 (pod)
978-1-945949-62-3 (ebook)

Waterfront Digital Press
2055 Oxford Ave
Cardiff, CA 92007

This book is dedicated to my dad, for always motivating me to write and having faith in me.

TABLE OF CONTENTS

BE WELL AND GO HORSEBACKRIDING OFTEN.

PROLOGUE

Sven held a bottle of whiskey in his armpit, his wife-beater tank-top biting creases into his cigarette-dried skin. He stared at Jenna with the red eyes of the devil as she gingerly creaked open the trailer door. His light gray and blond hair matted to his pink stubble. A cigarette hung from the side of his mouth.

"Jin, that is one damn creaky door. Ain't you ever gonna get that thing fixed?" He snarled out the words like spit onto her dirty linoleum floor. The cigarette waffled in his mouth. Her shoulders slumped forward and she frowned at him. Didn't the man see any positives in this world? She tried to reframe things for him. "Yeah, but I have priorities like you Sven." She moved his name around in her mouth, she liked the sound of it and wanted him to feel important.

"What the hell other priorities you got besides me?" He started to breath hard and stamp his feet. He was getting worked up.

"Um, none really if you must know," she faltered, almost choking on her words.

"No, you ain't really good about nothing are you?"

"I'm good about things." She felt small and inconsequential.

"Jenna why the hell can't you just shut up. I mean you don't give up do you?"

Jenna realized that there was nothing to say to this man. Disagreements were futile because he could spin genuine gold arguments out of scrappy hay. But she wanted him to love her and so she let him stay. She let him put her down over and over and he talked and talked until her ears rang and her heart ached. She realized she would get to work so tired she was like a robot. She could not fill her mind with other thoughts or do anything but cater to this man-beast.

"Oh by the way, Jin. I got a favor to ask. You can't say no, cause you ain't capable." He waved the whiskey bottle around. His armpit odor filled the trailer and the trailer creaked as he waved. "I got some things to drop by later. I got an old girlfriend who pissed me off something good. She's done for."

Jenna didn't even say anything. If she did he would disagree or start to argue.

"You know anything 'bout stallions?"

She didn't know what to say. Was Sven flirting or so drunk he wasn't making any sense?

She had never owned a horse and knew absolutely nothing about them except that they appeared strong-willed and large in size, just like Sven.

CHAPTER 1
PUDDLESCAPES

"When confused about your trajectory, pick a direction and walk. Eventually you will be told to turn around or allowed to continue."

– *Chief proverb*

Ashy little freckled African-American girl petted the momentarily self-contained fourteen hundred pound stallion that her ex-boyfriend Sven had left behind in her neighbor's pasture. The beast rippled with evil potentiality. It appeared that black oily snakes were rippling under the glistening horse's dark hairy flesh. The smell of sweat and anger emanated from its muscles to her across the pasture.

"Oh gosh, Jesus, Mary, and Joseph!" A lipstick-smeared cigarette fell from Jenna's tight-lipped mouth, a pink smear left on her chin and chest where it trailed too slowly to the ground. Jenna's blond hair stuck to her pale and pink moist sunburned forehead. The heat this time of year was like an electric blanket, cozy and warm, but co-dependent and needy, causing sweat to accumulate on her forehead and constantly matting her hair to her head. The only remedy was a rusted and paint-flaked window air-conditioning unit that rumbled like a car when in use. Only problem with the drad-blasted things – they always sold out at the local store by the time she realized she needed one. Her squinted dark blue eyes glanced out through the grid of the creaky screen door of her trailer home, and she shifted weight from one bulbous hip to the other. She quickly left her trailer for the adjacent field where the child and beast trembled. A fence about five feet high with healthy room for a human to fit through its large logs contained the pasture. Jenna's greasy sweaty hair burned as if it stood on end and she reeled in shock as her plump bloated body began to realize she might be saddled with more than a horse. She hoped to goodness that the child was a neighbor's daughter. No wait... then the death of the beautiful child would be her responsibility. She prayed silently that it was a mirage. That it was fake. That there was not a black child standing in the field next door with the monstrosity that had earlier eyed Jenna with the wild fury and hatred she had become used to from her ex-boyfriend, Sven, the man who had left this beast behind. Yes, this horse was very much like Sven and she hated the reminder. She cringed at the thought of that horrid large, ugly, demanding man. Her teeth gritted as she thought of the fat, needy sex, of the alcohol and form-aldehyde smell of the trailer when she desperately had tried to make him happy, at the times she had saved him from other desperate women. She remembered that he was like this horse, always shacking up in someone's pasture, eating all their food, and scaring them half to death. Wow, just like him – angsty too.

It was like Sven had left his inner beast behind. He had somehow given her the worst part of him, when all she had wanted was the best part of him. What a backward tradeoff, Jenna thought. This was her penance for loving someone who did not love her back. Loving someone who did not respect her. Somehow, she still cared for Sven.

The horse pounded at the ground and let out a great bellowing whinny that was probably heard down in Social Circle – two towns distant. He was a large sweating beast with shiny anger-laden muscles, dark brown eyes that she swore had a bit of the red trident of the devil in them and a shiny dark muzzle. His hair was full of knots and long and he was all male with large horse balls that swaggered back and forth from between his hind legs as he bellowed his manly zeitgeist. Clearly, the horse still had testosterone surging through his huge freakish dinosaur veins. He raised his head up high and his eye connected with her own. A shot of adrenaline seemed to flow from a philotic cord extending from the shivering quaking beast to her own body and Jenna found herself on shaky and knocking knees. She gripped her stomach as she started to sway like a ship on a stormy sea. She couldn't imagine how these animals had children. She felt a wave of nausea hit her and felt her brain lurching too in its small casing. The horse bellowed, bucked and then stopped and his eye met her own eyes again. He was a full four-feet higher than her, she thought. After all, who has a pet you have to look up at to see? And how do you control it or get it under control? Just how do people ride these animals? He must be some sort of anomaly. Riding this sort of animal had to truly be dangerous. She felt her thighs getting sweaty and slipping against each other and felt like she'd pass out soon if she didn't take some sort of action.

"I need another darn cigarette," Jenna proclaimed out loud to those names she had initially started the conversation with. She ran to the side of the fence nearest the child and was out of breath when she finally arrived, wheezing and slow, unused muscles swollen from the effort. The feral animal noticed the concern and plunged it's massive horse balls and moist dirty horse smell between her and the child. He smelled sweaty like grass, but also of the smell of anger, ripe and manly, like a locker room in the Amazon with an overabundance of aged socks. The girl jumped up and down and giggled a high pitched squeal, luckily not noticing what Jenna had noticed. Jenna wondered only fleetingly what a black child was doing in a mostly poor ignorant white neighborhood. That in itself could be a dangerous happening in this area where folks always wanted to think they were better than someone, when they weren't. She remembered the Jena 6 CNN coverage and winced. Why do we do such things? Who in their right mind would put a noose on a tree in the South. Didn't people realize how hateful it was? Was this child the byproduct of some sort of horrid act of racism? She wasn't sure how this thought could enter her mind at a time like this, but often we think of everything we can, when given a new situation we aren't used to.

"Oh gosh, don't move," Jenna thought. "Stay still!" Jenna shouted. The beast reared up on two feet and swaggered his head in a circular pattern. Steam dissipated from agitated nostrils. Again his eye connected with hers. A ripple of shear terror ran through her heart and she felt like a small but fat plastic toy encased in concrete. A little being mired in this gigantic world. She shook her head free from the horse's bedeviling trance.

He danced around the girl who started to sniffle and her face darkened and reddened at the edges. "Uh, be nice horsey – pelease." The girl was wearing a very smudged up jean jumper that clearly had not been washed in a long time.

"Don't- Don't taaaallllk to it!" Jenna was caught frozen in a state of horror. Her knees were no longer shaky, they were now pudding. Sweat trickled out of every pore. Her brown skirt and off-white tank top were soaked with fear and dread.

The horse danced to the other side of the pasture and jumped and reared as it went. The sun shined along his back and he too glistened from the moisture. Warm wet fur patches could be seen around his stomach, upper legs and a white patch of congealed and remoistened white foamy sweat between his back legs. Jenna felt like a solitary hardened can of gelatinized gravy and still couldn't move, like she was now stuck in the concrete again. The little girl sniffled some more and tried to rub her eyes dry.

"Come here little girl. Come on."

The little child was confused and wasn't sure what to make of the horse who was nonchalantly eating grass while keeping a serious focused eye on the two of them. Jenna thought about the situation and quickly jumped the fence. The moment her leg lifted over the invisible dotted 'crazy horse' line above the fence, a neuron ignited in the depths of the beast's skull and he made a mad and swerving turn – the whites of his eyes showing high as he came tearing after her pounding the heavy earth and sending grass and dirt clumps flying high into the air. The child was momentarily stunned by the furious horse and then cried out and ran to Jenna. The two met and Jenna with babe in tow lunged out of the way and back through the fence hitting the ground just before great hind legs swathed their shadows with ill purpose. Jenna tasted and spit out grass and a clump of dirt was stuck on the child's neck and smudged on her face. The beast had meant to do harm to Jenna. He felt he owned this little girl.

The child's kinky light brown curly hair made a halo out of her cherubic face. "Thanks lady, I'm Josie." The little girl hugged her sweaty leg. She noticed how much more beautiful the child's skin was compared to her own, since her own was pimpled with acne and hair follicles.

"Sure, hi Josie." Jenna brushed herself off and looked the child in the eye. There was a wildness there, but also kindness and fear. Poor thing. Left here with this mad animal. Or something like that. She probably had something to do with Sven too. She looked a little bit like him too, despite the obvious difference in skin color.

"How'd you get here Josie?" Jenna smiled at the child but gritted her teeth a little. She didn't need more responsibilities.

"Man said you'd watch me. He mad." Josie tried to make her face look angry when she said the word 'mad.'

"Oh, what's the man's name?" Jenna tried to act nonchalant.

"I call him Sven Sven, but he go by Sven. He my daddy. I don't think he like me."

She made her way back to the trailer with the child with one hand on her calf. The hand was cool on her sweaty skin. Jenna took the child's hand in her own instead. Her leg was too sweaty to be reassuring and she feared the child would trip and fall. "Let's get away from the horsey." The screen door creaked a rusty entrance hello as they entered her trailer and subsequently slammed shut, metal slapping against metal, a more welcome greeting than usual to Jenna.

And so after this near-death experience and in the trailer with the little girl safe that cooler evening, Jenna started to write an ad to sell the monster or get rid of it somehow. The buzz of an electric mosquito trapper zinged in the background. To hell with Sven. Why did she have his crazy horse anyway? After all, she'd bailed Sven out a couple of times and paid for the window he'd broken and only received a total of $5.00 back from the asshole. Her hair fell forward in a fair swoop and her head fell exhausted to the keyboard, beads of sweat sliming the interface of human to computer, some dandruff mixing in the air. The little black child, cherubic and yet a responsibility no less, looked sober and solemn. She was obviously Sven's child. She had his face shape and his curiosity. Her skin was dark, but lighter than some African-Americans. Why hadn't Sven gotten her pregnant with a child? She had many hopes for Sven when they had met and in the first month. There was no love there now. Was there love anywhere? There was a sigh there somewhere. It got lost in the shuffle, she thought, with an obese sigh. Good lord...Her life was downright depressing.

Jenna had few friends and ambled through life trying to impress each man, much like her friends had growing up. They had all gone their separate ways, either married or somehow singular but always pining for a step up through marriage or a relationship with a man. She remembered one man from before Sven. There was Harry who was short and had a Napoleon complex. He was always trying to be better than everyone else, always competing. Harry had dark hair and liked to don a simple goatee. He was known socially among the town as a cowboy. She had known Harry when she was young, petite and pretty and she had been a trophy to him. She was always there when he was playing pool with the guys, she always dressed up and put on make up for him. She remembered the tight t-shirts, the bras with extra padding, the jeans that left creases on her abdomen after she took them off. Harry treated her like she was a dimwit and had no interest in Jenna's life. She remembered trying to start interesting conversations with him. At one point, Harry had fallen asleep while she was talking to him, sitting in his Mustang at a bar he wanted to wait to go into.

She was merely an accoutrement, like his wristwatch. There had been other men but sadly Jenna could not remember them because no one had lasted as long as Harry and Sven.

She remembered how she had been attracted to Sven's anger and angst. He was muscular and tall and menacing yet when she first met him, he had seemed like a big teddy bear. He had worked in a steel factory just north of town for a while but his temper had seemed to get the best of him. When she met him, just before he was fired from his job, he had been grumbling into a whiskey with a cigarette on the table at the Bitter Bar, a local establishment with shady low tables, cigarette smoke covering almost everything and everyone, elderly men bent over drinks nodding at patrons. Despite the name, Bitter Bar was a biker bar known for its whiskey. Jenna had been there with a ditzy blond friend of hers from high school named Candy.

He had asked her, "Why do you suppose Jimmy gets all the damn promotions? He has no guts, no strength. He was a fucking accountant before he went into metal!" Sven pounded a fist on the table. Later that month, Jimmy would tell Sven about his family and then politely ask Sven to stack his products in a certain way and Sven would explode, momentarily choking Jimmy while pinning him to a wall. Jimmy had to go to the ER because the choking made him pass out. It would be on that day that Sven would be fired. Jenna sat next to Sven mesmerized by his bulging moving muscular arms, his six-pack abs that peaked through his t-shirt. He had one keltic tattoo on his left arm that rippled when he flexed his muscles. She had wanted to run her hands all over him. She had commiserated with him, told him he was better than Jimmy. He had taken her to his apartment on that day, the month before his anger would spiral him out of control. They had made love with the lights on, Sven staring at her chest and massaging her thighs as he seemed entranced with the newness of her. He would pass out after they made love and ask her to "please get out now" the morning after they made love. Sven did not appear to be a morning person. She also worried that she had done something to anger him or had somehow grossed him out.

When she would go to pick up Sven after she had bailed him out of jail, the sheriff would utter to her under his thick breath, "Come on Jenna, you can do better." Then he'd pat her hard on the back like she was a big guy. "You're a tough one Jin." She grunted and pulled her coat tighter against the dry cold. Tighter against this life she'd chosen. She knew she had taken a U-turn somewhere and gone backwards by mistake.

"Tell me 'bout it." She'd say to the policeman as if she was a bystander in her life as well. She had to think about her next nicotine hit in order to dull her repetitive low-life oblivion. At the same time, she felt like there was more to her life. She felt there was more she could do if she put her mind to it. Sven did pull her into his personal Dante's Inferno, and she did know better. What was she doing? After all, hadn't she been cute once? In the old days, the policeman would stare and the implication of "you can do better" would imply that the policeman was offering up himself as the alternative. Jenna had no such luck these days. Afterall, work kept her so busy that the big lug cup full of Pepsi, a Grande French Fry and Grande Chimichanga were all the pleasure in the world she could find. Unfortunately, the instant transfer from stress to mouth to thighs hadn't made a correlation in her mind just yet.

You see, though she knew he was all wrong for her, Jenna's ex-boyfriend had heaved himself onto his cranky motorcycle and skipped town a few days ago. According to the little girl, she was Sven's daughter so he had left Jenna with a child from another relationship. She had saved the child and almost gotten killed. A huge and angry horse beast now wanted her dead. She noticed Sven's nasty greasy hair gel that really just perpetuated his slimy Harley rider look next to the kitchen sink. She thought maybe he'd left a leather jacket tattered in the barn, smelling of cheap women's perfume, but that was it. The man traveled light, and she wondered as she sucked in the gritty tasteful smoke from her Kent Light cigarette, where else had he traveled?

Jenna wondered if she now had a habit of picking up wanderers, given that her brown eyes had set sight on Sven. He was a swarthy drunken Swede with a penchant for bar fights and a thick hyde. Lately, the night always ended with a trip to the police.

Sven would come out of jail looking like a big ol' grizzly bear with a five o'clock shadow and heavy under eye sockets drooping under his beet red-veined eyes with permanent frown wrinkles that looked like exaggerated tattoos stubbled with dirty hair. He'd mumble nothings for hours and then fall into a babbling drooling stupor much like a toddler after a late dinner mealtime. Later after the sleep he'd be in a horrible mood, trip over everything, have a constant headache and she'd look forward to his next trip to the bar, the wonderful 'pre-jail' peace.

When Jenna had double-mortgaged her trailer to fork over the bail money, she'd wondered why she was with him, but somehow she chased the ghost of the past. He used to show up at all weird hours, calling and passionate and full of mad love for her. She remembered once she'd called him and dared him to be there in five minutes or she'd lock the door. He was there in ten minutes and broke her window to get in. They'd made love for three hours, consumed two bottles of

Jose Cuervo Tequila and smoked a bowl of weed. The next day she felt stale and used and sick like she'd danced with the devil a little too long. Women problems abound, but that night, that high, that feeling that she was the object of affection fueled her tolerance of this obese, unattractive pink pimply smelly beer consumed man. He was so egotistical, every time he became drunk he got in a fight with her about involving other women in their affairs. Jenna drew the line at that and so he talked about it and she indulged the oral fantasy, but not the tactile fantasy, since her morals were somewhere, just out of reach with this fat babbling nemesis that she found her unhealthy obsession with.

And the window he broke cost her almost as much as her rent on the trailer. It was a special window that was now out of stock at Trailer-mart, so she'd had to pay twice as much. In her neighborhood, you didn't leave windows broken, otherwise you were liable to lose more than just your broken windowpane. When she'd asked him to help her out with the payment on the window, Sven had grunted with gravel indifference and gave her $5.00. After that, she didn't see him for a month. She learned that maybe it was best not to ask him for the bail money either. A month later she had brought up the topic of bail money.

"Sven I can barely afford all your bail money." His stubble looked razor sharp. Blond greasy hair fell over his forehead.

"Why'd you pay it then?"

"Maybe because I care about you?" Jenna's eyes felt moist.

"I don't need this fucking emotional mumbo jumbo Jin. You pay it or you don't."

"Can you chip in?" Jenna looked at him questioningly, holding back a tear.

"What? You think I'm a bank? Hell no. Don't pay it if you kin't afford it." He had slammed down a fist. He looked at her like she had said something ridiculous.

He had muttered a few cuss words and jumped on his motorcycle and avoided her for a month and a half.

Another time Sven had called her in desperation. She hated him just as much as she felt she loved him. His voice sounded gravelly on the old phone. "Uh, hi, you there Jin? Git me the fuck outta here. I got this crazy women who says I'm the daddy of her child. I need you to talk with the authorities and Jin, what the fuck you doin' on the phone. Get me the fuck outta here!" She'd politely asked him for the address. He'd lost his temper trying to remember the address then told her "get off the phone and get movin'! damnit!". She'd missed his drunken hugs and that sometimes he seemed to like her afterall. He would tell her how misunderstood he was. She would sometimes stare at him across the bar before she walked up to him. His pensive anger was somehow attractive to her, but she would hate how he treated her later. He would sometimes be kind and laid back, watching her like a prize cat when they'd first met. He'd smile at her and tip his hat but she could also see the simmering anger in the pools of his irises. She pulled out a cigarette and maneuvered it with the door to go pick him up. When she got there, a woman ran out and threw a bottle and her underwear at the car.

"Whore!" the woman screamed at her. "Liar! Fuckin' biaaaatch!"

Jenna winced at all the stuff coming out of the crazy lady's mouth and the way the woman swaggered along like a man and Jenna started to get indignant and scared. "You don't know me!" Jenna tried to yell, but it was uttered as more of a hoarse chirpy whisper. She hoped her car didn't get too messed up. Her car was already old though and had taken far worse abuse.

The woman was skinny and didn't look pregnant, but was obviously drunk. She wore a T-shirt that had been ripped into a tank top. Jenna could see her breasts through the side of the shirt and her skirt was ripped on the side. It was a light-washed jean skirt. The woman was also missing a front tooth and had a semi-mullet that went down past her shoulder blades. Her hair was feathered in the front. Jenna thought to herself, "the dream of the eighties is alive." Her tank top said, "Lynard Skynard Rules" on the front of it. The woman managed to get in Jenna's face and told her with alcohol and cigarette breath thick with the smell of salty redundant sex, "I'm the mother of this man's baby." Spittle made it's way onto Jenna's face from the gap where a tooth used to be.

Jenna just repeated into the gap, with desperation and hoarseness, the, "you don't know me" mantra.

Sven turned the ignition and shouted to Jenna. "Get the fuck outta here damn-it! What the fuck you starin' at? She ain't no baby daddy!"

Jenna glared at him, but hit the gas in fear of the lady with the attitude (who now attempted to straddle the front of the car) and lack of dental hygeine. Sven was complicated though. Later he'd tell her he wanted a bottle of Cuervo and wasn't she a dear for gettin it. But the pursuit and imbibing of alcohol seemed his only nicety. And this person – who was she? This crazy woman needed some focused healthcare. Perhaps a dental implant and some mental health services?

When he was sober, there wasn't very much interest in Jenna. He'd bring her a camisole and she'd slip it over her fat body and he'd seem somewhere else, and she'd grimace herself back into that safety of fat clothes, something to cover that mess of Sierra Madres thighs that seemed to have sprouted from her lack of movement. He would pass out when it was time to get anywhere anyway.

Sven was intense and despite his lack of brain cells lost to alcohol, he was intelligent. Nothing was perfect. There was always a hair on his proverbial lens. His glasses were not rose-colored. They were yellow and tarnished and he was never happy. His hair was greasy. His belly was bear-like because he drank to much beer. But the woman he was with had to be perfect. She had to embody everything he asked for. And Jenna was no longer a biker babe. She went from the shapely Christie Brinkley to Roseanne Barr in one year's time. He had this posture, like he wanted to say, "Jenna, what the fuck happened? I settle down and you SETTLE down (implying fat settled to her butt) too, but not the way I imagined." She wasn't sure why he still spent a little time with her.

And she now associated him with so much anger. She knew in her heart of hearts that he saw her as this blubbery mass of inhuman thing whose sole existence was something akin to a beer koozie for him. She knew it was happening and the way he wasn't there. Well it didn't matter. She had a little brat from God knows where and this gawdawful horse that eyed her with a certain flair of the devil. She eyed him back from the kitchen with wary suspicion. He'd chase the cat around the pasture like he was going to kill it and in the height of his fury, he'd turn a brown lit eye upon her with nostrils flaring and veins popping. The connection made her grit her teeth in horror. Didn't these animals belong in zoos? I mean you don't just decide you want to own a 1,300 pound animal do you? She wasn't sure what to do with the horse. How do keep these animals and why hadn't it run away yet?

But the new and obviously abandoned daughter had something to say in the matter, she thought as she finished up the ad to sell the beast. I mean the child liked that crazy horse. Oh geez all the more reason to get rid of the beast. She suddenly had this horrible vision of the horse chasing Josie around like she was that poor cat. Veins popping, eyes bulging, hooves afloat, mane wild, and boom, Josie flattened like a soggy cow patty in the field. Afterall, the animal looked hungry too.

"Uh – oh." Josie, dark curly mess of hair, chocolate smooth skin and beautiful almond shaped eyes looked down at the vat of milk that she had just dumped on the floor. She started to sniffle and Jenna saw it coming. "Honey I just got to find somewhere to put this ad. That horse has got to go. Don't make any more messes! I mean come on!" That added to Josie's sense of chaos in the light of spilled milk. But she was wondering – where do you put an ad for a horse? She hadn't seen any in the papers at all. She didn't know anything about these large animals. This was the first time she'd been near one.

"Horsey go goodbye?" The child looked at first confused and then the decision to cry and carry on had been decided. Her kinky hair frizzed at the thought of it all. Rain dropped from her face onto the floor – a mini drizzle storm in a cheap creaky old kitchen.

Jenna got a paper towel from the cabinet and went to wipe the floor of milk.

Josie pointed, "puddle-scapes." She uttered and stuck her thumb in her mouth and stomped out to the horse, through a flimsy screen door. Jenna followed, generally perturbed, interrupted in the current task, disturbed, and though a child is quite different, she was immediately reminded of an out of control dog that she was determined to adopt that had eaten everything in the house twice (once regurgitated, and the second time digested). She'd buy a new couch, bam! gone – eaten from the supports up. And she had been a waitress for crying out loud. This dog would shoot out of the house like a bullet and Jenna would wish the dog had a permanent leash attached to him. Instead this dog would go find the biggest most ferocious mangiest looking canine in the neighborhood and pick a fight with him. One vet bill later, they'd go home and both get some rest. The dog got run over this past summer. Jenna was bothered that the dog's death had given her some relief. This kid was like that dog running after that crazy horse, but here was something more fragile. A child doesn't just have scars all over. A child doesn't go to a vet. A child…Jenna remembered that she need to buy some cigarettes. She wanted to forget the fucking child. She was never one to think of having a child. What with her bad choices in men, love of drink and smokes and her crazy hours at Super-Mega-Mart. She worked six days a week. Two months ago they had gone on strike for not getting overtime, and the place had shut down and she'd lived on just french fries for two days and swore off the union for life. Even though she believed in the bigger picture stuff, she thought sometimes life just didn't work that way. You put up with the unfair long enough and things got to get good. You know?

But things were getting progressively complicated with the hasty retreat of this most recent asshole love interest. One year and the man leaves her with more baggage than she has time for. Jenna stuck a foot in the ground as she kept a few paces behind the girl. The girl giggled and pointed at the horse who seemed to show a fraction more respect for this little thing. He proceeded to eat grass like he didn't care. No eyeing, no bulging veins, no wild fury. The girl leaned on the fence. A smile, a reach, bright eyes. Jenna didn't want a replay of the previous episode of killer horse.

"Josie, don't you –"

She reached over and grabbed this strange girl, so different from herself. So beautiful, yet scary, and pulsing with energy. Killer horse ate some grass closer to them with more ferocity.

"The horse pretty." Josie exclaimed with certainty. Teeth poked through a half smile, more of a look of confirmation. Dad probably hadn't taught her as well as he could have. Most of what he had taught her was sad. Stuff like gettin' him a beer. Putting on the helmet so he could hoist her onto the bike. Toughening up for the road. Learning how to be Christie Brinkley someday, or maybe in Josie's case, Halle Berry.

Jenna pulled her light hair into a knot with a rubber band behind her head. "When the heck is your dad coming to get you?"

Josie looked confused and then looked up again, hair easing to one side one eye higher than the other, lips pursed and cheeks dimpled, "He say not long."

"Momma die. What that mean …?"

"Yes, I know. That means Momma is never gonna see you again. You've got to behave now," Jenna said, realizing that this child didn't have a concept of what death was yet. Children always had to justify these things, and her dad just didn't seem like a pillar of moral guidance into intimate questions of life and death. Sure he was intense and he had this image and this life. Riding free on the hog with the guys, meeting new girls in new places, but that was what he was serious about.

Jenna wondered if Josie understood anything about death. She worried that Sven expected her to be this child's mother. She had no time for children. She was no mother, no shining example of morality. Didn't this child belong in school anyway?

Little Josie didn't like her answer, but instead of crying she was quiet and cross.

She was unlucky to have been born to such a father, but also probably gifted in some ways because of it. This man was as ADD as they come and darn selfish about it too. Motorcycles were his passion and nothing else stopped him from it. They were processed byproducts. Sure he had the bread, but he didn't need cheese and women to him were like cheese. Nice to have in your cheese sandwich now and then, but not necessary like the bread part. The grit and the bugs flying in your face and the pavement. Getting a farmer's tan cause you hogged it from Tennessee to Maine in one day straight. She knew well the hangovers of impracticality, but when she was high on life with him, she felt the free spirit of roaming and she loved the feel of the wind and the earth on her cheeks, the changing scenery. Jenna had decided she liked these things about him, liked the freedom of the road, but with too many of his bills and too much responsibility he was unable to master made such a life both impossible and impractical. Though she liked his sense of freedom and adventure, she didn't like how it made him treat her, his own life or others. His life embodied her best times, but also her worst.

She remembered the time he had taken her to Savannah, Georgia. Her knees were numb from the vibration of the motorcycle, her arms sore from holding on to him. He hadn't had a helmet for her and told her he preferred to see her hair 'go up all Medusa like.' He told her she was beautiful and wild with his expressions and his stare. He had left her in the motel for most of the night they were there, but she loved him and she didn't care. He was always roaming. She had loved having the bed to herself too. To where he had gone she did not know, but she accepted his wildebeast and let him do what he needed to. Had he met Josie's mother that night when he hadn't come home all night? The night they had made love and then he had left? Was this man perpetually wandering?

And so now the byproduct of the byproduct of his irresponsible lifestyle was this beautiful child. The child had Sven's face shape, Sven's look of defiance, and his wild-eyed curiosity.

"What will we do with you?" Jenna eyed the little girl and frowned. She wasn't sure how to care for a child.

"Last girl Sven leave me wit had blond hair too." The little girl stared at the horse, stared at Jenna.

With a dramatic flair she hit the ground with her barefoot toes. "Horse do that." She exclaimed. Josie definitely had the cute act down to a tee.

"Yep" Jenna winced. Flattened into small change. Didn't seem right for a little girl, that while annoying, was cute. "Don't go visit that horse no more Josie. The horse could come hurt you if he really wanted. He could kill you."

Where were her shoes. She had new teeth coming in and so she talked with a lisp.

"Well let's head back to the trailer. You dropped the milk. Gosh darn-it, you need somethin' to eat. And gosh darn-it where are your shoes?" Jenna was trying to be friendly, but wasn't sure why she should be.

"Chocolate pancake." The little brat smiled a little, questioning Jenna with her look. Her tooth gap showing between new teeth.

"Pop-Tart?" Jenna asked. They had had a five for one special at Super-Mega-Mart and Jenna thought she could save some money by having some breakfast foods on hand. She had fought this old lady named Gurdy for them in the supermarket. Gurdy worked in produce and she had been eying those Pop-Tarts for a week. But she wouldn't buy them. And Jenna was respectful for that whole week. She steered clear of the scrumptious red raspberry frosting variety that she liked to eat after being all warmed up in her toaster. But gosh darn a week had passed and the old lady had put that special variety in her cart at the end of the night when she shopped and then she left it in the panty hose aisle and Jenna would have to carry it all the way back to the breakfast food aisle. Why can't people just put the stuff back where it goes? Especially someone who works at the place where other folks always leave stuff randomly around. As a result of people like this, Jenna had to stay late and scour the store for the virtual Easter egg hunt amalgam of indecisive near purchases. But anyway, right when she got to the cash register the old lady tried to grab it, saying, "Jin, I dropped that somewhere, thanks for pick –"

"No Gurdy, you done left it in pantyhose. You can't have it now." And she smiled respectfully as she grabbed a magazine pretending to eye the new J-Lo and Matt Damon romance. Gurdy's white still hair and green cross eyes burned holes through the magazine. She regarded Jenna with newfound disrespect. Jenna felt a little bit guilty hoping maybe there were some more pop-tarts for sale in stock.

And tonight was no exception of problematic people. There was also Mr. Hunt. He would ask on every fifth purchase – "Jenna kin you scan that for a price check but don't ring it up. I got ta stay under 12 dollars today. Not sure I can buy it right now, if ya know whats I mean." Then he'd have to just have to buy something that'd put him over the edge, couldn't figure it out and leave the whole line scuffling their feet and eyeing their watches, or pretending to read a magazine, when they were just really impatient. I mean millions of years of evolution and now we're waiting in lines and counting change? What's wrong with this picture? And by the way, what mean jerk leaves an unruly child on an ex-girlfriend's doorstep? I mean you read about this stuff in the Enquirer when you're in one of these impatient situations, but really, that stuff usually only happens to famous people right?

Well, she would agree with most people on the evolution stuff. Weren't we better than this retail work stuff? She had worked at Super-Mega-Mart for 5 years now. She didn't accumulate close friends but did get long with her coworkers just fine. They were like a dysfunctional family that she could leave at the end of the day. Light banter and polite hellos and goodbyes marked her days though sometimes she listened to Helen who worked at the check-out counter complaining about raising 5 kids and working non-stop or Betty in produce who had to have a double mastectomy and then recouperate quickly so her husband could have his surgery. Though she did not love her job, she liked it and she was grateful to have a job as there were not other entry-level jobs available. The economy in her town was deplorable and it was even difficult to get a job at the Super-Mega-Mart without an associates degree. She wondered if there was better work out there than Super-Mega-Mart? She was grateful for the work. If she didn't have it, she realized there would be no Pop-tarts, no Hershey's Kisses, no Entemann's pistachio green stuffed candies to eat slowly, no out of season dollar ninety nine christmas lights to decorate the trailer, and no instant orange juice to sip out on the deck, while you shooed away all the pesky skeeters, wondering if you'd be the next poor person to get meningitis. Why is it rich folks never get meningitis?

"Yah, Pop-tarts." Josie headed for the trailer in decided determination. Jenna pondered what to do with the horse again. The devil horse's eyes popped up from the grass to eye the flurrying dart of a child and then he went to the fence and poked his head over it. He let out a snort, turned his butt towards her upon realization of Jenna's attention and he went on lawnmowing with one angry red eye on her. She was wondering what the horse would eat and remembered that Sven had said, "give him sum hay if he runs outta grass." He was lookin a little skinny already. How does grass fuel such a large animal? Do horses go on Atkin's Diets? She didn't really know what the diet was but knew it had something to do with meat. She had gotten a pamphlet in the mail from the American Beef Association. "Eat more beef and live longer" it said "with the Atkin's diet," and there was this doctor who looked kind of overweight and bloated promoting it. She would have tried it, but the proof is usually in the pudding. And this guy had had too much of it so to speak and then she heard on TV that he had died of a heart attack no less. She really couldn't afford too much meat anyway. She imagined the horse would need a lot of something like meat. Did the horse want to eat her? He had chased the cat. Hell, he had chased her. She emphasized in her mind that Josie should not play near a hungry twelve hundred pound animal. What if this was the story behind so many missing children. "Twelve hundred pound horse found to have consumed at least eight children." That would be a good story in the Enquirer. This would have to be Jay Leno's horse or something. To this though, Devil pounded the ground and ran to another part of the pasture. She felt the little earthquakes his hooves made by driving his large feet into the ground as he pulled away.

The screen door shut with a creak and Josie shuffled into the house. Her skirt was a dirty yellow and her knee had a scrape. She also had a smudge of dirt on her face. "Dear, you look like you could use a bath." Josie gave her that confused, I'm gonna cry soon look since she had verbally mentioned a bath. She also needed to wash the child's clothes.

Jenna ambled over to the cabinet and put a Pop-tart into the toaster on low. It popped 20 seconds later and she plopped it onto a plastic green plate. She also put some Tang into a plastic cup that was turning a dirty color on the top of it with some cracks. Need new cups, she thought as she placed it in front of the little girl.

The child proceeded to stick small pieces of Pop-tart into her mouth very fast. Jenna had to slow her down by having her use a fork. Instead of helping, it added to the mess on the floor, since every other piece sailed over her shoulder in her desperate attempts to eat something that she had obviously been lacking in. The brown tabby cat was licking up some of the milk, but eyeing the Pop-tart pieces with indifference and disgust.

"Don't be throwin' food over your shoulder!" Jenna had almost had enough of this little brat. Sure she was cute, but couldn't she do anything right?

The little nuisance lifted her head in angelic clarity and look confused while she chewed as fast as she could.

"Hungry!" the child exclaimed muffled by food in her mouth.

Jenna wanted to reprimand her but instead forced her to slow down by helping her with the fork to mouth ratio that was statistically not working before now. The little girl bucked the trend and instead sent more pop tart flying into her lap and not quite making the mouth landing. This made Jenna more angry and she tried to force her to slow down.

"You need food. You got to slow down damnit!"

Josie turned red and cried and sputtered out chunks of pop-tart.

"I miss mommy!"

"Oh for crying out loud!" Jenna let the little girl continue to eat too fast and wished she had bought more cigarettes yesterday at the Quickie Mart. The crying sputtered out lost in the concentration of the fast eating of the pop-tart.

She had to figure out what to do. Should she call Child Protective Services? It crossed her mind to do so but she worried that she would just make Sven angry and possibly violent to both her and the child. Her shift started in exactly three hours and here she was saddled with two large responsibilities and two small messes. One responsibility was quite physically large, the other large in theory. And the messes seemed to grow with each new event...

Jenna decided she needed to try to unwind from the eating event. So she sat on the sofa for another hour watching the latest episode of the Bachelor lost to the mindless numbing of the television. These were reruns but she loved the way the guy treated the girls so nicely. It was a nice way to tune out from the world. Josie sat on the other side of the couch and eyed the butt of the horse through the window. She was also staring at the road and sniffling. Did she like that big hairy smelly man that she had to call dad by birth? Did she miss him? After some commercials about the Slim Fast diet, one of the particularly skinny women went in the hot tub with the bachelor. "Out of all the things in the world," he asked, "what do you want the most to have?" Perfect makeup didn't move on the blond girl's face despite the steam of the whirlpool. She smiled a delicious cheshire cat smile and sat back in the big tub. Bubbles bubbled up against her slim golden collarbones and her shoulders seemed to relax when she made a decision on what to say. This glimmer of thought hinted to Jenna that she had something to hide or that the answer to the question deserved extreme reflection.

"I would say…" she hesitated and then blurted quickly with a questioning lilt at the end, "World peace."

"Good call!" the football player-like man answered with gusto and sidled over to her side of the tub. The woman smiled in triumph and the man handed her some champagne that seemed to twinkle. The surface of the tub water even sparkled. "For you my lovely. Is there anything else I can get you?"

Jenna sighed and Josie crinkled her nose and emphasized, "Boys are weird."

Jenna's lip perked and she chuckled to herself. Sven had never ever asked her if he could get anything for her. Did he even know what champagne was? Well, once, but that was to go get a dirty movie at the 7-11. She didn't know that you could get dirty movies at convenience stores. Sven had called her ignorant and she had cried later on and bought a women's magazine that had "how to please your macho man" on the front cover of the magazine. It hadn't been very informative or helpful. It recommended baking a cherry pie, and giving 'your man' a massage. Sven hated massages or any type of touching like that (unless it was two to three minutes of foreplay) and he hated fruit unless it was candied or in cream flavor. He loved ice cream.

"At least we get to eat a Pop-tart, unlike Barbie." Jenna laughed and jiggled to the sad little girl.

The phone wasn't going to bring any answers. Since the advent of the Internet, no one called and she hadn't a good computer for access to the Internet. So she'd opted for the phone. She had to call folks sometimes. And the monthly fees for access to this electronic thingie stuff was just too much on top of everything else she needed. She'd have to figure out how a modem worked first. The guy at the store had asked her if she had one when she'd asked how to get on the Internet. She'd imagined a big antennae sticking out of a scrappy computer, bringing in Internet signals from the heavens. She felt religious just thinking about it. Did God create the Internet?

With hopeless determination mainly driven by the girl's interest in the horse, and the lack of her confidence in said killer horse as a babysitter, Jenna picked up her dusty phonebook from under the silverware drawer and blew on it before she opened it. Dust tumbleweeds danced in the air and the smell of cheap perfume wafted by her nose. Mama was listed first. She dialed the number with anticipatory fear and remembered cleaning up her mother's rotting throw-up from the couch after the Christmas party at her trailer last year. It had been lime green due to the drink she had been drinking. Some sort of Mountain Dew drink with green food coloring. She couldn't eat green food after that very often without thinking about it.

"Yeeeesss." A grumbly graveled voice answered on the other line. It was like the phone was attached to the old lady's head and she had woken up from a deep sleep in her grave. Jenna almost thought she heard a tombstone move over.

"Hi Maw." Jenna paced the floor with her eye on child and horse. "I got a problem."

"I got an answer," the lady chuckled raspily through the chink of ice cubes on the staticy phone. "And the Injun man here has another answer."

"Maw. Why –" Jenna stopped short of treating her mother like she was this child she pictured in front of her. She wasn't sure what her mother was doing with an Indian man and wasn't sure she wanted to know. She hoped her mother could attempt to babysit. Afterall, Jenna had no one else she could think of to turn to. "Listen, can you babysit?"

The line was quiet. Her mother's heavy breath was caught in a vacuum of confusion and alcohol and phlegm. Her mother coughed some phlegm up, appearing to struggle to understand her daughter's request. "What the blazes? Jenna you got knocked up while we ain't seen each other?" The phlegm sounded like it was spat into the phone.

She wasn't sure calling her mother was a very good choice, but she had no other options. Jenna sunk down into the couch wishing to disappear.

Josie eyed her with suspicion and then stomped into the kitchen. She proceeded to attempt to open the refrigerator with little success. A second tug sent the fridge door violently open and two eggs slid out of their round egg-shaped nests and onto the floor. A virtual egg-nog had been created with milk, pop-tarts and eggs. Not so festive this time of the year. And no fun to clean up. And a mess the girl or she would be likely to slip and fall on. Heck, that was how her Uncle Skipper had had to get two new hips. He'd opened the refrigerator too fast, slipped on some orange juice and rolled down into his living room from his kitchen. He called it the "Epic Roll." He wasn't found for 3 hours and by that time the doctors said both hips needed to be replaced. Or at least that was Skipper's account. He had highlighted to Jenna that it wasn't due to his morbid obesity. Uncle Skipper moved to Mexico 4 years ago "to retire."

"Look girl, darn it, sit on the couch there." Jenna spouted in anger. She was reminded of the wild Golden Retriever again as the girl started to sing to herself and amble in the other direction. "Now please."

Josie stared up at her with big eyes and sat on the floor in front of the TV. Little girl and bigger TV. Her silhouette shined through the images of the bachelor in yet another scene where he, the All-American quarterback, with perfect teeth and sharp angled jawline, treats the girl to a picnic in a city park with champagne and strawberries and she acts like a Miss USA throwback, bleached hair, fake tan and all. At least he was nice to her.

"Maw you gots to help me. I got a shift in three hours. Don't you work at Mr. Convenience in the mornings now?" The feral horse let out a high whinny and throaty neigh, bellowing at the sky. It galloped from side to side of the pasture.

"Well, yeah I used to. I retired finally. And I smell awful. Haven't showered in gawd knows how long. Sounds like an unruly brat. Too old to be yours. There's a horse there with you too?" She still spat and the chink chink of ice cubes was in the background. "Gawd I need a drink. Is that a monster I hear or a horse?"

"Damn horse is in the neighbor's pasture, right outside the door here. Neighbor said he can stay there for a few months. Sven asked him. Sven left for good. He left a note. Awww maw I haven't talked to anyone in a year now and everybody done moved or got married. I don't know what to do. I didn't expect this. I didn't plan this." She sniffled and wiped her nose. "Maw, I got to pay the bills. I put a second mortgage on the trailer for Sven's bail and then he left too, and –"

"Girl, you got to figure out that you're too nice to these men. They smoosh you like an ant and then expect you to wait around on them. You got fat again I seen when I spied on you at Super-Mega-Mart. When you gonna take care of yourself? Always get fat with a man ... ." She chuckled a raspy giggle. Jenna's fear, she felt, was appropriate. Her mother had a way of soakin up all of her self esteem, stomping on it and then throwing it back at her. It took her time to recover. She remembered her mother both before and after alcohol, or rather before she knew her mother was an alcoholic and after she knew her mother was an alcoholic. Her mother was always the lift of the party, always making her feel one of a kind as long as she wasn't drunk. When maw drank she was crude and slurred and direct. She said what was on her mind. Jenna worried that she would become like this, become unkind and uncaring.

But when her mother wasn't drinking she was one of the kindest most compassionate people Jenna knew. Jenna remembered that her mother used to be a nurse, used to work with homeless people, helping them get back on their feet. Her mother would get phone calls at all hours asking her to come to work to help. When maw would take Jenna to the store, they would thank her mother for getting them off of drugs and alcohol. They would tell little Jenna 'if it hadn't been for your momma here, I wouldn't be alive today.' Then they would smile at her. Unfortunately, maw's job had been too much for her. She had worked many double shifts and worked extra hard to support Jenna, but at some point, her spirit was broken, cracked. The reason Ms. Higgins worked with this population was because she had a background of alcohol and wanted to help those who were mired in it, get out of it. But when Pa Higgins was diagnosed with pancreatic cancer and she was trying to hold him together and manage his pain before he died and keep her job, it was all too much. She almost lost her home due to medical bills.

At the time, the insurance company had called his cancer "a pre-existing condition" and they had difficulty getting his treatments covered. However, given his cancer, he passed quickly prior to the most expensive of the treatments. She spent some time paying off his medical bills, but towards the end of it, slipped into a deep and everlasting depression and turned to alcohol. Jenna was older and less dependent on her but it did instill into Jenna a sense of work ethic and fear for drugs and alcohol. At the time Jenna had started to work to help her mother. She had dropped out of high school to help her mother.

Jenna remembered the many times her mother had tracked her down when she was an older teenager. Her mother had threatened her boyfriends and frankly, all of her friends that if Jenna ever turned to drugs or alcohol she would 'track you down and hang ya by your hides.' Nobody was going to be responsible for another Ma Higgins so they fervently protected Jenna in the farm community, Jenna also aware of her mother's background.

When sober, Ma Higgins always provided her encouragement when no one else would. No matter her mother's depression or illness, Jenna came first. But Jenna could not handle her mother's slow decline, her mother's binge drinking episodes and seeing her mother face down on the coach sleeping in her own spittle. Her mother changed into a mean, direct argumentative alter ego when she drank. Ma slammed doors and told her she was 'not a good daughter.' She told Jenna she was 'a wimp and woos.' Their relationship became abusive to Jenna. Because of her mother's alter ego Jenna had great difficulty caring for her mother and far greater difficulty seeing her mother disintegrate before her eyes. Jenna had moved into her trailer, far from her mother. But she would always help Jenna and Jenna would probably also always try to help her.

"Maw."

"Yeah girl, I'm coming. I'll be there in thirty minutes or so."

Jenna knew she had an unhealthy attraction to Sven but couldn't break free. She also knew in her heart he was bad for her but just wasn't ready to let go. Sven had really hurt her multipe times. Sven had been a first class jerk. She remembered the time she had been out with Sven's friends at the big Hog tavern and all his Harley friends were bragging about women. She had told them how much she liked Sven and they had all laughed and said that Sheila, Nancy and about six other girls liked Sven too. Jenna became very mad and left Sven a message about this. How could he date all these people? It had become Sven's silly joke – pathetic joke to turn his answering machine into a receptacle for it. The message said, 'Hi, Shirley, Nancy, Jenna, Michelle, Jackie, Alexa, Bernie and Bertha, I can't come to the phone right now, cause I'm with one of you ... in bed. Leave a message. Beeeeeeeep.' She had been so mad. She heard on the television that the difficult men had small wee wees and drove big muscle cars, like Hummers or old beat up Mustangs. It was what Oprah called, 'overcompensation.' Maybe she should just let it go. Afterall, she had quite a few distractions already.

An hour and a half later, Maw Higgins opened the screen door and fit her mop of bright red hair and mountainous thighs through it. The trailer creaked and heaved a little bit upon her entrance, seemed to move more than she ever remembered it doing so and the smell of whiskey and body odor was almost overpowering. She wore a bright dress that seemed to envelope her whole body like a an oversized pillowcase that had dirtied with overuse.

"One of these days a tornado is gonna come by and whip this thing up, and the insurance will allow you to get a new one." She pointed a fat finger at the little one, "that's the girl? The little dark-haired thing over there? Don't look nothin' like I pictured Sven. Sven was a black Swede? Is there a such thing as a black Swede?"

The little girl was positively frightened. She looked like a permanent wall fixture never to be moved. She had moved sideways until part of the window covering were draped over her. She was trying to meld into the furnishings.

"I don't bite yet. Need a bath, but your lady here has to go to work and I had to hurry."

The little girl tried to amble away more. Appearing to think if she didn't make eye contact, she didn't exist. "Not my lady" the girl stammered pulling more of the old window treatment over herself to hide herself. "Where Sven?" Though likely afraid of Sven too, the child appeared more afraid of Ma Higgins.

"Sven done left for now. Ain't that right Jin?" Ma Higgins stared at Jenna. "We need to call the police. You can't keep cleaning up after Sven! This girl needs to go back to her family! Surely she's got family!" The little girl seemed to wilt with this statement.

Jenna took a deep breath in. "Momma just give me some time. Please momma. He'll come back." She knew he would come back to her.

Her momma put her hands on her hips and stared Jenna down. "You serious?"

"Serious as a still cast iron pan, momma."

Ma Higgins shook her head. She said in a low tone. "Ok, I'll give you time, but if he doesn't come back we need to do something. Can't always stand by and watch your life go down the drain for someone else."

Jenna winced. "Well, I got to go. Maw you know where to find everything. I cleaned up a mess near the fridge and it's kinda sticky, be careful. And that child does not go near the horse, ok maw? No matter what, the horse stays there," she pointed. "And the child stays here. You ain't gonna drink too much right?" She worried about leaving the child with her mother but had no other choice.

"Go to work Jin. I'll have a talk with her if she misbehaves."

"Yeah, ok."

"How in the hell did this one turn out black. Sven was black? You messed around with a black man? Well, I got myself an Indian, I suppose."

Her mother had forgotten their earlier discussion she thought. "I'll explain later if you can't figure it out. Ain't nothing wrong with black folk." Jenna's mood wasn't very good.

She gathered her things and brushed her hair again and pulled it back into a rubber band and put on her t-shirt and pants and her button that said, "Hi, my name is Jenna, and I'm pleased to help you today." Yeah, I'm always pleased when I have to work a 50-hour work week just to get by. She was happy to have insurance with her job which is why she stuck with it for so long. With her health not always so good, she needed to make sure she could get to a doctor when needed. But the truth is, she couldn't afford to get sick. The deductibles and co-pays broke her budget. And the management gave her attitude if she called in sick anyway. That makes me real pleased. I'm pleased when you buy $40 worth of junk and still can't make up your mind about what's more important: your baby's diapers or a tub of ice cream. I'm pleased when you're fighting with your husband in my line, holding everything up and keeping me at work late. I'm pleased when I just ate a tomato sandwich and received an alert about possible E. Coli in the tomatoes. I'm even happier when your blood sugar gets dangerously low and you fight with me over somethin' stupid. Jen pushed opened the screen, looked back at the child, looked at the horse and opened the old Chevy door. It made a different groaning creak and its heaviness was apparent when she slammed it shut. The car was musty and she remembered that she needed to give it a good cleaning too. The sun was starting to hide in the horizon as the day was starting to get dark. Sven had left some food in the car a few months before under the seat and she hadn't cleaned it out quite yet. It reminded her of him in a really messed up way.

Time to work under the bright lights, she thought as she headed down highway I-91. She knew some folk at work who couldn't see so well. Did the bright lights cause it or help it? She was sure she should probably forget about that question. It was the least of her worries at the moment.

She had a horse and girl – two new additions to her now complicated life. She was just hoping that Sven wouldn't cause any trouble. She was also hoping her mother would quit drinking. She hoped that Josie was safe with her mother and also hoped her mother was safe with Josie. Would her mother keep Josie from the horse? She hoped so.

CHAPTER 2
MAD SWEATING BEASTS

You cannot really tell someone's character until after they have endured great duress. If they are able move on, trust them, if not, you move on. (Character shows up best when tested.)

– Chief proverb

Jenna pulled up in the smelly dusty oversized Chevy and grimaced about the long trek ahead – how many years of evolution to find yourself dragged around a sanitary Clorox nightmare under flourescent lighting with every type of bleached ass wipe and chloridated cleaner on the face of the planet? I mean they had 60 different kinds of bathmats... Well anyways, Jenna dragged herself through the self-opening doors and into the light – like a tunnel of normality into sanitary-ville. Follow the light, follow the light...

"Jenna, gots a spill on aisle 22. You can leave your purse here." The manager had a long handlebar mustache and glasses that seemed to meld into his face like a plastic nostril addendum. He reminded her vaguely of Mr. Potatohead. He gently grabbed her purse and frowned at her as if to say. "Get in shape, girl. Hit the ground running."

"Yep. Gotcha Greg." She adjusted her nametag and gave him an enthusiastic half smile and pulled herself, thighs bobbing, minus purse to the scene of the spill crime. She went by candy bars and the goofy music that played at the Hallmark stand. She knew the shortest way, which was through Automotive, with its new tire smell and straight to cleaning supplies. It looked like Windex had literally exploded when it hit the floor. No one was in sight. Dontcha love it how the customers never take responsibility for things?

"Yo Jenna, Greg asked me to bring it by. I just had a spill on 14. Some kid left an open ice cream bar and it melted and this lady went flying when she stepped on it. It was so totally cool like in the cartoooons!" A zit-laden tall lanky teenager with glasses and a plaid shirt with rolled up sleeves worked at a soupy mixture of grime and Pine-Sol in a wheel-barrow tub with a large brown mop. He wore his jeans high enough that he was sometimes made fun of in the store. She put the mop over the floor and worked it in and then dried the mop by using the automatic latch to tighten part of the mop and squeeze the wet out. Then she ran it over the Windex again. The Pine Sol and Windex together did not make for a great smell. She sniffled and almost gagged. She came close to vomiting but she was able to hold back. The boy was Jimmy. A local red-headed kid who was attending the community college. He still seemed of high school age and appeared to have not yet hit the testosterone stage. She didn't see an overly apparent interest in babes, but then she wasn't attractive anymore. He acted nothing like the swarthy Swede she had mistakenly loved. Maybe when you go to school you have elevated interests?

At the same time, Jenna missed being attractive. She daydreamed sometimes about being a contestant on the

Bachelor. She would be her younger self, Jimmy's age, all gangly and off-kilter in terms of hormones, but buxom and doe-eyed. She couldn't imagine Jimmy being attractive but imagined a more executive, responsible version of Sven – also younger, before drugs and alcohol had turned him into a bear. He would choose her among all the women. In her daydream, Sven would end the contest early, pointing to her saying 'I already know, she's the one.' She was lonely for sure, but Super-Mega-Mart at least provided some social activities for her and got her out of her trailer. She was appreciative for the work and the kindness of her coworkers.

"Thanks by the way." She nodded Jimmy's way.

He grunted in agreement and left to find more entertainment. She knew his shift would be over soon.

Jenna reflected on Mary Sue, who was blind in one eye and demented in the other and on her monthly visit, they actually had an employee follow her around the store to catch anything she might knock down in her path – I mean the stuff was stacked so high too. Greg referred to her as a liability. He had wished to them privately as he pulled on his mustache that she would go to the Social Circle SaveMart that Super-Mega-Mart might be putting out of business. Jenna liked the old lady and enjoyed the entertainment of following her around and the old lady steadying herself on something ridiculous, like a display shelf of motor oil. Jenna had stopped following her and actually walked with her arm in arm – it was easier than watching her every move. It was Jenna's social time with Mary Sue. Mary Sue didn't make a lot of sense but her stories always started out interesting.

"Jenna did I tell you about the motel that blew up ski high? Someone was making drugs there!" It was something Mary Sue had seen on the news.

"I didn't hear about that one, Mary Sue."

"Them drugs, so stupid." Mary Sue reached out to a loose box to try and get her balance, the box was next to a tire. Moving the box would have knocked over twelve new tires.

"Nope, don't lean on that, here, take my arm."

"Just trying to make your life interesting Jin'." Mary Sue giggled.

Did she know what she was doing? She knew the old folks home was probably pretty lonely.

"How long is the van leaving you here for?" The Park Commons van usually dropped her off for an hour or two so she could take her time.

"Oh, two hours today." She had a list written out with things scribbled and crossed out. She saw "snow tires" on there and wondered about it because Mary Sue didn't drive. She also saw "squeaky dog toy."

Mary Sue seemed to read Jenna's mind. "I think I grabbed an old list by accident."

"That's ok." Jenna knew what Mary Sue usually bought. "I'll take you to the chocolate aisle. Then briefs and paper towels."

Mary Sue smiled, "What would I do without you Jenna?"

"Everyone seems to do better without me," Jenna disagreed.

"Hmmm. Sounds like you're letting the world get you down. You're better than you think you are. We all have potential." Jenna doubted Mary Sue would agree if she knew what was really going on in her life.

After getting all of Mary Sue's items, Jenna brought her to the register where Mary Sue paid for all of her items, then she sat her down in the cafeteria. Mary Sue ordered a Diet Coke. She noted to the attendant "None of that non-Georgia

Pepsi stuff, I only drink Coke. You can't fool me." Just when Jenna thought Mary Sue was making sense. But then she ruminated, Coca Cola did taste better than Pepsi, she thought. She remembered hot days on the porch drinking Coca Cola from glass bottles that sweated because they were so cool. She missed those days. She felt good back then she thought, or maybe she just forgot the bad times easily.

Leaving Mary Sue in the cafeteria heading towards Automotive on her way back to recheck the spill to make sure it had dried, Jenna was stopped dead in her tracks by the sight at aisle 16. It was the section devoted to rifles, hunting supplies, and next door, auto supplies. She saw her Harley man, Sven, filling a rifle with small bullets. He was definitely painfully sober (or maybe just a little drunk) and very unhappy. His grizzly demeanor was angry and grumbly and he frowned, cheeks laden with stubble and a red glare was apparent on chapped skin too. He was not in a good mood. What do you do in this situation? Her heart rate increased and she hid behind the shelf. "Breath, Jenna, breath," she muttered to herself. She was suddenly nervous and feeling fat and not real happy with such a confrontation. He could do something bad, real bad. He could... kill somebody especially if he had had a lot to drink and was on a downward slope. She could tell when he was overcome in a fit of anger.

"Uh, hi Sven." She moused over too him and cowered in great fatness.

"Jin. Get the fuck outta here." He made a great sweeping motion and some bullets fell onto the floor. "Chink chink chink" then they made a rolling noise as they made their way to the counter on the slightly sloped floor.

Jenna contemplated the situation and left Sven for the manager. She nearly tripped over a child who was running out of the children's section into the Hallmark section.

She made an abrupt stop in front of the manager. "Uh Greg. My ex-boyfriend is in the hunting section and he's got a rifle. Now, he's not –"

"Jenna, he's been buying rifles here for quite some time. He always seems angry." the manager perused his mustache with his hands and straightened his glasses on his nose. "He's just going to go shoot some deer and get over his anger. That's all. Take it out on hunting, ya know."

Jenna shifted her weight to the other foot. "No. No he ain't. I get the feeling he's angry and he was supposed to leave town for a while. I think he might be in trouble with the law this time Greg. He ain't himself lately. He's more angry than normal."

"Jis avoid that area of the store Jin." He ain't your type is the message that danced in the manager's eyes. The manager eyed her with a toothless smile. It was a dirty little smile and Jenna groaned internally. Her stomach dropped at the thought of it all. Gross. Really gross. She knew he liked larger woman since she'd heard it from Gurdy who'd worked with this guy for some twenty odd years. All she could think of was that nasty oily mustache tickling her face, if that would ever happen, which it wouldn't. Some customers shifted uneasily nearby. One pretended to read a magazine while she waited in line. Jenna went to cash register number four and unlocked it and waved a lady over. The lady stopped her light perusal of Oprah's greatest secret love and rolled her cart to Jenna. The lady was buying charcoal, lighter fluid, XXL pink minky pajamas, some soap, and a matching pink fluffy bath mat. Jenna liked to think about how the items people bought shaped their lives. Usually women that bought pink items lived alone or lived with a good tolerant man. Pink was not usually a favorite color of local men.

Jenna was thinking about how the women on the Bachelor often wore pink. The Bachelor seemed tolerant of this.

"GET THE FUCK outta my way!" A sweaty pink-faced, scraggly blond haired six-foot Sven ambled angrily down aisle 10 towards a cash register, sweat flung from his whiskers. Super-Mega-Mart saw all types come through. Perhaps the unwritten policy at this Super-Mega-Mart in a rural location was a rude customer had to carry on for a bit longer before management would do anything –that they knew that most of these angry type customers were just blowing off steam and would be out the door in a matter of minutes. He looked like a a broad bull ready to pummel anyone wearing red. Except he appeared pinkish red, steaming through his nostrils and ready to hurt someone. He donned a leather jacket and black pants that barely covered his pregnant middle. His belly button peeked out. His head lowered so that the great bags under his eyes shook with anger and it accentuated his grizzled stare. She knew his breaking point. Despite his look of sobriety, she guessed he'd been drinking. Maybe he cut it with some Red Bull or something. Maybe he needed medication. No one moved despite his declaration. His wispy blond hair was sweaty and greasy and matted to his head. "Jin check me out now. I'm going to your place to shoot something. A mistake. What the fuck was I thinking?"

The horror of his statement hit her smack in the belly. She didn't like the horse either, but really do you just shoot an animal in cold blood? She wondered if the Manager was taking things more seriously now. Could he hear Sven?

"Sven?" Time stopped around her and she saw Sven and she saw her mountainous self of uglydom and was mad at how Sven saw her and how he hated her and how he targeted her too.

"JIN. What the fuck am I paying for this?" He shoved his way to her counter.

The manager looked cross and his nerdy demeanor mixed with country cowboy and a shot of redneck. Her manager had a habit of not calling security, thinking he could handle these things on his own. "Sven, I don't care whatcha do when ya leave, but pay for the damn thing or we'll add it to your record. We got cameras, Sven. Jin will ring ya up." The manager seemed to tremble a little and his lips trembled a little bit in determination. His moustache shook in concentration. There was a reason why he was manager. These stupid people coming in and messing with him. He wouldn't stand for it. The manager picked up a phone. "We got a 911 at the registers at the front." A 911 actually had no real meaning but perhaps her manager knew it might scare Sven into behaving. Why was he dragging his feet and letting Sven get away with this? By the way, Jenna would have to pay for Sven's tab, not Sven.

Sven sweated and steamed and he seemed to snort. Sweaty mane billowed into the air. He flung a credit card at Jenna. It smacked against her nametag and hit the floor at her feet. The sound of a plastic card hitting the floor. The manager looked stunned. Her heart hit the floor. The smell of Sven was aggressive and it was horrible. She ran the credit card and it came up "unauthorized" on the machine.

"Sven..." She handed him the credit card. He growled and pulled out his wallet from deep within his pants. It was like he was tapping into the zen of maintaining his anger. Sweat and greasy hair flung into the air and Jenna thought of the horse. big nostrils flaring – hatred searing from angry eyes. She trembled when he handed her the next card. She would have paid for it herself, but he was buying a rifle. I mean how could she pay for something that he might use to ruin or hurt with? A killing thing. She wouldn't mind buying whatever he needed and getting a 10% discount... She wouldn't really... but maybe he'd shoot somebody. He still looked handsome to her. She couldn't deny that she still cared for Sven.

The next thing he pulled out was a wad of cash. Mostly ones and fives, but he finally pulled out $85 worth of them and he flung it at her in what seemed like a large spit of cash and the waft of alcohol, cigarettes and grubby cash flew in the air that hit her face. Green danced in her eyes for just one moment. He had told her a few months ago that he kept the cash on hand for strip clubs.

"Just go Sven. I'll keep the receipt." She used her calming voice. It made him angrier.

"Just go? Really? Like I listen to you?"

Fellow customers stood by, silent, holding their breath. Some had meandered off to be far from this scene. Jenna wanted to hide. She was embarrassed.

"Jenna. I'm going to shoot that fuckin devil." The dead serious look in his face was premonition for something hideous and deadly. "That evil woman pissed me off! –"

Store alarms sounded, bleating out, making customers duck, some hit the floor. The manager, for only the third time in store history, had called security and stated this was an emergency. Jenna heard him in the background. She knew the police were on their way.

"You wouldn't." Jenna instantly lost care for her job. For her place. For herself. Biology played some factor in this.

Sven wanted to shoot the child she took care of.

"Sven she's innocent."

Sven shuddered and he was bloated and drunk and angry. "Ain't nothing innocent, 'specially a bastard girl."

The manager had a taser in his hand, pointed at Sven. "Jenna you do your job and you stay here." He seemed like some distant voice – like the manager was the angel on her shoulder and the devil was Sven, angry and red in all his lack of glory. She was afraid the manager might make a mistake and tase her. He had bad aim with most things, but thought highly of himself.

"Sven!" She stammered. Peace turned into some sort of contagious anger.

Sven darted the manager and slammed through the automatic doors, which stuck open, and his sweaty alcohol cigarettey smell wafted her way again and it hit her like a smack in the face. And this time she hated it. She hated everything about him. Was there love there? No more. How could she love a killer and of a child no less? A beautiful child. Josie's importance took on new meaning to Jenna as she tromped out of Super-Mega-Mart like a zombie. She had hated the child at first, but now she surged with motherly instinct. She realized Sven had likely used the child's mother just like she had used her. She realized how beautiful the child was and how sad this situation was. She shifted her hatred to Sven. How many times had he used her? How many times had her let her down? Her mother was right. Jenna winced yet again. Maybe Mary Sue had a point too?

"Jenna you get back here or you're fired for good." The mustache drooped and swayed as the wind from the automatic doorway swooshed past him. He righted his glasses and frowned sternly. "You'll never get a job in this town." He seemed like a little voice to her. The sound of the jammed automatic doors chopped his voice up.

But, she apologized anyway. "I'm sorry Greg, but Sven seems like he's going to kill the little girl who's staying with me. I've got to protect her. I promise I will be back."

She heard Greg the mouse in the background. Wait – mouse? Manager ... Oh well. She tromped over the rubber mats, hopped into her car and sped down the road after the motorcycle muffler sound that seemed to bleed through town. Not something Jenna normally did, she pulled a cigarette out of a carton she'd bought earlier at work just before the spill on aisle 22. She felt kind of free, but more scared for life than anything else. She took some puffs and her wild imagination started to wander. She imagined Sven confronting her drunk mother. Sven knocking over the trailer. She even seemed to imagine him driving and shooting that poor girl or her mother. Shooting what he created? Or would he just burn the whole place down? He certainly hadn't been the poor woman that pushed that beautiful baby out. He'd merely had the pleasure of inseminating her and that was no cause for death.

No cause for death was the name of a trashy novel she had eyed a day before in the books section. It looked particularly interesting, but Jenna wasn't sure she could read it. She had never gone past 10th grade reading and she had found English to be more daunting than most tasks in life. The funny thing was that the English teacher was such a jerk and her mother had said that math was so hard and Jenna had liked Ms. Gray, the math teacher, so much that she did well. Good teachers to Jenna made for good grades and she didn't believe any one subject was better than the other, but some teachers were better than others for sure. So she'd left the novel at the store not wanting reminders of her bad English.

The car sputtered along 1-95 and time was too slow for her. She sat at the red lights for what felt like eons. A child's life! She hit the side of the car with her fist and just sped through everything. The patience that she had accrued for so many years dissipated in a rush of sadness and anger. Jenna was fearing for the child's life. This poor innocent thing.

When she hit the corner of Woodle and Edemark Road, a cop saw her run the stop sign and he sidled in behind her. His light went flashing in red and blue and he turned his noise up load. She trembled at the mere thought of a cop following her but knew she was close to him. She breathed harder. She felt like she was running a race. She had to get there. She couldn't stop she had to keep going – this poor child. She was falling into a sad fearful mantra for this child. The best thing that could happen was the cop would get to her house and her drunken mother would be passed out on the couch and Josie would be asleep with her after having had some wonderful milk and cookies. Yeah right – like that'd happen! The poor child had probably been smacked up side the head a few times.

Finally after what seemed to her like an hour or more, Jenna's ten minutes of driving had come to an end. Sven's Harley was there with his glasses over the wheel and rifle tag ripped off and thrown on the grass. The neighbor's old beat up pickup truck stood bright red against the green grass as well.

She stood for a long second and fear shot through her every pore. She oozed the smell of death and the smell of longing and she anticipated the worst. The fact that she hadn't stopped for the cop sent a shot of fear through her veins. The cop opened his door slowly after having written down her tag number. He sensed something weird and pulled his gun from his holster.

"Ma'am. You mind telling me what's going on?" The cop was handsome with 80s glasses and a general CHIPS look about him. His hair was feathered and one lone crumb was on his cheek from his afternoon at Denny's eating some fried okra and mashed potatoes. The waft of it hit her nostrils, she found herself salivating over the man. She started to sway a little. "Ma'am?" The cop knew this lady was not going to get in trouble for what had happened, but he felt it was his obligation to figure things out. He could sense her fear and her nervous energy as she visibly trembled in shock.

And he thought she was beautiful the way she seemed strong but so vulnerable. A stray blond hair was over one of her eyes but he resisted moving it for her. He worried for her and her family. He knew something was wrong the moment he had noticed her run the stop sign. She just didn't seem like she did it with ill purpose. He had noticed her car sputter and struggle and then the neurons fired telling her to keep going and he saw tears in her eyes as she blew through the stop sign, her face red with fear. He thought maybe scolding her would just worsen the situation. He wanted to help this beautiful woman. He wanted to provide some more strength for her. She was what he thought to be the perfect height and maybe she could lose a few pounds but she had a cherubic face with pouted lips and deep blue eyes. He worried that he would spend so much time staring into those eyes he wouldn't be able to help her. He shook his head and tore his attention to the scene around him.

He politely put his hand on her shoulder to say, let me go first, then went fearlessly in front of her and creeped into the trailer. He felt a shudder when his hand touched her shoulder. It was like electricity and chemistry; a longing stirred within him but he suppressed it with thoughts of duty.

They walked towards the trailer together silently, "Hello?" He called into the trailer. Jenna fell in behind him and the trailer creaked when she heaved into it. She noticed his shoulders and the way he carried himself. She smelled aftershave and fabric softener and thought how kind he was to her. He was careful and deliberate also doing his best to keep Jenna safe. She wasn't used to that. She wondered why he hadn't been mad at her about running the stop sign. She didn't get pulled over much, but when she did most cops were really mean about it. She smelled like Super-Mega-Mart and she worried that this could repel him, but he stayed close to her.

The impact of the situation hit her with a pound in the chest. Jenna started to cry and couldn't even start a sentence. She was instantly embarrassed and wondered if it was due to her shyness as well. She found that she liked this man and at the same time was in a horrible situation. She tried to tell him what was happening but couldn't figure out where it was happening. "Svenl -b try..buy..gun." She stammered. "b–t–g ... " "Svenb ba Svenb" Oh well. Find everyone. Find them now she thought. She blushed a crimson red.

The cop read her mind, put a hand on her shoulder, rubbing it lightly, again with a calm smile and started to creep in the other direction hand on gun holster and small square metal radio talkie on. He had turned off the walkie talkie to keep silence. She thought she saw muscles in his arms that flexed when he had helped her. His jawline had firmly hardened as he turned from her.

When they stepped together outside the trailer, she saw figures standing out in the field. The lawn looked like a crime scene to her. She knew something was amiss. The cop sensed it and he called for backup.

"Folks...uh...we got a ten-twenty here. Copy." The cop had also seen the rifle in the big man's hands. Sven was a shadow against the evening sun. The light reflected off of his sweat beads and sun glinted off the rifle. He wasn't angry anymore. He was sad and Jenna was even more sad. She cried more. The cop made a hand gesture of complete control and signaled her to go behind him. He smelled clean and safe. He talked over his radio again. "The man we got a ten-five on is the same man seen at the Super-Mega-Mart and has made his way to the Shady Meadows trailer park. He is located at five five one Shady Meadow Trace in the pasture by the gate. Roger out."

The cop turned to Jenna, "Greg has got to stop thinking he can handle this stuff himself." The cop was referring to Jenna's Manager. This was the cop's second run in this month with someone who had bought a rifle at Super-Mega-Mart.

Sven had actually bought the gun, but Jenna wondered if perhaps his manners had triggered some sort of alert. Then she remembered the 911 over the intercom. Someone had called 911 and alerted the police of a possible problem. They had ID'd Sven from the cameras, despite Greg.

The cop pulled out his gun and shouted from his car, "All of you, put your hands up and get on your knees!" Sven did not do either things he was asked to do but the cop kept his gun on Sven. The cop then walked calmly up to the scene. Something had gone awry. His stiffness of being made Jenna nervous because she knew that he knew that he was about to witness something terrible. Sven, Mama, Josie, our neighbor Joseph, her Mama and an old weathered man all stood looking solemnly at the horse that trembled on the ground. The cop seemed to swell with his own anger and sadness. He was a tall man about 6 two or so and seemed to have a heart. Most cops had egos, and this man seemed to have a heart.

"What happened here?" The cop ran military-like to the sad form of Sven and removed his rifle forcibly. He hand-cuffed him and put him in the back of his car with the doors locked. He gave Jenna the rifle and and instructed her to lock it in his car trunk. Shooting a firearm while drunk was unlawful. She looked sadly down on the sight of the once noble creature. Josie cried but was silent and sniffling a whole lot. She looked tired and had baggy eyes from crying. She was probably better behaved given the evening's events. The neighbor and cop and a man dressed like those Indians you see on television all congregated over the horse. Ma held onto Josie and kept her from going to Sven in the cop car.

They were discussing something and had all come to a conclusion. This conclusion ended in the cop looking very solemn and sad and putting his hand on his holster. Jenna knew that they felt they had to kill the creature and put him out of his misery. She swelled with a future cry and her eyes welled up. He pulled the gun out and aimed.

"No no no!" Jenna ran out and stopped him, standing between his gun and the beast.

He looked her as if to say "Dang it, now you talk." She pleaded, she begged, she cried. Great wells of water formed in her eyes. The cop put himself between her and Sven. Perhaps this was to help the situation.

The horse lifted his head and let out a soft knicker and squeal. His great ribs seemed to shake and swell up and down. He was breathing, but it wasn't easy. Blood oozed from a wound in his back leg just above the joint.

"He had bad aim, huh? It looks like the horse is suffer-ing though." The cop said in a manner trying to lighten the mood, yet sorrowful for the pain of the animal.

Jenna removed her shirt and tied it around the horse's leg. He tried to kick her but realized how much it hurt and stopped his leg in mid-flight and sighed deeper into the ground. He just breathed harder and knickered some uneven notes in response. Clearly the horse was rattle, down for the count. "Can someone please please get a doctor – some kind of doctor. Anything damn it!" She yelled it mostly at the neighbor, but also at everyone else who seemed to be lollygagging around. "We have a hurt animal here!"

Mama let out a rasply gurgle. "Jin. You don't got no money to pay for that."

"Well, I hid some cash just in case – like for school someday or something. It was left over from the money I'd gotten for Sven's next bail." She sighed. Mama wasn't real good at letting her get further in life.

"You need a vet." The neighbor pulled a cell phone from his pocket and punched in some numbers. "Yeah I need the number for a large animal vet in the Wilkinsville area please." He stood there and listened. Why is it that lots of poor people have cell phones, but not much else. "Ok small animal vet is fine." "They don't got no large animal vet listings." He let us know while he was waiting. The lady had obviously started talking again cause he nodded his head and grunted lightly. He had been connected. "Hey Dr. Barnhart." He stooped over the phone. "Got a horse over here. Not sure what to do. There were no large animal vets listed. Ok, great. We was worried we couldn't find no one. Yep. Yeah that'd work. Nearby? Oh that's helpful." The neighbor hit the end key, the phone made an end jingle and he slipped the phone back into his back pocket where his old leather wallet made a square shape against his jeans. "Someone's coming out Jin. Hold tight."

"Jin I thought you hated this animal. He's downright evil." Mama was putting her opinion where it wasn't needed as usual. Her hands stood on her enormous hips as she peered upon Jenna, she swayed a little bit from the three or four rum and Cokes she'd had that evening. Ma liked her alcohol.

"Ma, I'm too tired to fight with you right now." Jin sucked in her cheeks and sighed. She needed some coffee or a cola or something. Sometimes she wished things were more complicated like she could fight with her mother and have her would improve, but now she wished things were less complicated. This was one helluva day! Her mama looked big and old and deflated. She was wearing some blue mermaid earrings and her hair had obviously been died such a bright red, Jenna noticed it now more than ever. Her skin had that old weathered look of a wise woman – but Jenna thought differently about it – was probably the result of too many cigarettes. Today Mama was wearing a t-shirt that asked, "You lookin' at me?" and Jenna wasn't quite sure of the significance besides the whole De Niro thing. Mama's boyfriend the Indian man was as quiet as she ever knew anyone to be. Her mother had called him while she was babysitting and so he had arrived to help her. Her mother referred to him as "the responsibility half." He wore crisp blue jeans and a white tank top over old leathered skin honed to a perfect dark brown by the sun and many years of hard labor under it. On his head he wore the headdress she'd seen on television as well as some color on his face that might have been tattooed there. His silence was significant and pregnant with meaning, and it hovered like a stale smell. They both seemed sober and caught up in the fervor of the moment and yet lost and still. A moment when Mama wasn't drunk. A moment when they were all together. A moment of fear and dread hovered over all of them.

And the dread increased with each minute until the fifteen minutes later when the vet showed up to help this huge animal – twelve hundred pounds of fury laying in a wilted clump in her neighbor's lawn.

"Dr. Barnhart?" The neighbor walked up to shake a hand.

"I'm the vet. You're fortunate I have some horse experience. Not many large animal vets out here so I do it every once in a while." The vet seemed of good nature, but he was instantly sobered by the sight of the animal. He appeared in his late seventies with a starched brown plaid shirt and tan work jeans with suspenders. Mature and deliberate, a thinking man's veterinarian. "Oh no." The vet took his cowboy hat and put it over his heart in a moment of respect for the great animal. He had brought what looked like a tackle box and it had his name inscribed on the outside of it. He put it on the ground and pulled out a stethoscope. He ran a hand over his bald head behind his glasses and put the stethoscope around his shoulders and onto his ears. He listened to the beat of the horse's heart. The horse flinched and moved an eye to take in the situation. The vet gently flipped back the horse's lip and looked at his gums. "A little pink," he said with clarity. "That's a good sign."

He started to untie the shirt from the leg and looked at the wound.

The doctor looked up at all of us. "I'm curious as to why the horse is lying down? They don't normally lie down unless they're colicing or near death, or really content. I'm guessing he's not content."

"Sven punched him in the head after he shot him," the neighbor said it with sadness.

"That'll do it." The vet sighed. "Well I do know one thing."

Everyone waited for the vet to say the next thing.

The vet looked at the cop. The cop sized up Sven, handcuffed in the cop's car and just kept looking on without saying anything. His strength was in his ability to assess the situation on his own. Sven sweated profusely and his smell wafted down from the car was just short of downright disgusting. Toilets smelled better than he did and that was a longshot. The vet pulled out a long metal instrument and started to assess the wound site. "Pretty nasty shot. Luckily it just chipped off some bone instead of breaking it, but did some major and permanent muscle damage. And the poor horse may have some brain damage. Who punches an animal in the head?" The man eyed us all with seriousness. The cop winced. Jenna winced. The little girl sniffled. The Indian man pulled his pants further up and seemed to think of something far away.

Two other cop cars pulled up onto her lawn with lights flashing. They proceeded to talk with the cop on his radio. They had taken a long time, but Jenna knew from the newspapers that their police force was underfunded due to multiple city issues.

He pulled out something – Jenna didn't know what from the wound site and then he proceeded to stitch it up nice and neat. He then pulled a syringe from the tacklebox and injected a clear liquid into the horse's neck. "This'll help him get some rest after that episode of abuse. I won't talk about what preceded this incident of animal abuse, that's up to you all to work out. But I would watch him for a good week and make sure that the wound stays clean. Maybe Sven here shouldn't own any animals... Also here's some bute." The vet put some large white pills into a bottle and then rested them in Jenna's hand. "Don't go crazy with the bute, it's bad for their intestines. But do make sure he isn't in too much pain. And call me if you need something stronger for him. Right now he's on heavy duty stuff. But he should get up pretty soon. Horses don't normally sleep on their sides unless they're really comfortable or really sick. He needs to heal though. And I'd recommend that you keep an eye on him." The doctor's hand motions followed his thoughts.

The doctor closed up his case. "Oh and one last thing." The doctor stood next to Jenna. He smelled a little like Bengay and mothballs. "Make sure and mix a 1/4 cup of oil in with his food. It'll help in case he does colic. He's not feeling so well right now and he's in pain – this is a prime time for colic. And colic is quite a problem – it kills every horse different and no one can cure it."

"We don't feed him, he eats grass and I guess maybe he'll get hay too?"

"You WHAT?" The vet was incredulous. He eyed the horse and sighed. "Eventually once he's feeling a little better, you'll need to start him on a pellet food like Horseman's Edge or something. Keep the protein at about 10 percent right now and work him up to one scoop. Start out at 1/4th of a scoop and work him up to it. For the next few weeks though, lots of medium-grade hay and1/4 cup oil in the evening. His feet'll need some trimming too. This'll all cost some money you know…" He said this eying the dilapidated trailer.

Jenna reeled at all her new responsibilities.

The cop moved Sven's rifle. Then the cop seemed to think about the rifle. Jenna watched him from the hill at the pasture. The cop was contemplating something and acting like he was going to walk back up, but then he talked to one of the other cops who had rolled down his window to talk to him. The cop stared at Jenna with something important to say, but she thought she was too far away –what was he hesitating about? She saw kindness and help in his brown eyes. Then he closed the trunk and he drove off with the Swede in the back of his car and a train of cop cars. They all turned on their lights so they'd get back faster with this hoodlum in the first car. Jenna hoped Sven felt real bad and she knew he'd get out soon too. Hurting an animals wasn't a huge offense – was it a huge offense? Who knew… That man was a walking disaster.

"That's $100 for the emergency visit and $100 for the bute as well as the stuff I gave him to settle him down. So, it's $200 dollars please."

"Can I pay $100 now and you can bill me for the rest? I was so scared. I wanted him helped. I had no idea Sven would do this."

"Not something I'm in the habit of, but you have quite a situation here. You can pay me the rest, but please don't wait too long. Your address ma'm?"

She provided him with her address and phone number.

"Ok done." He said as she walked back to the trailer to get some of her savings out of the cookie jar. She pulled out a wad that had been counted as a $100 and brought it out to the vet.

"Thanks," he said as he folded it into his leather wallet. The wallet had puppies etched into the leather.

The vet took a piece of paper out of his toolbox and circled some things on it that made no sense to her. He then handed it to her. "Keep this for his records. Oh and what's his name?"

Jenna looked around at everyone. Sven was gone and it was his horse originally. Now that she paid it's bill, she felt that if the horse lived it was hers and so she should name it and probably eventually sell it, but what to name the thing. And she doubted she'd get attached. It'd be nice to get some of that bail money back. She remembered how much it had hated her when she first set eyes on it. She was sure it still hated her. The episode with the child has changed her for sure. "The horse's name is..."

"Akwënöi" the old Indian man said with particular emphasis and direction. It was the only word she'd heard from him since she knew him. What a weird name for a horse too. She would've asked him what it meant but she was afraid he wouldn't answer. Hell, she was afraid he might answer too.

"Ok." the vet raised an eyebrow and somewhat confused at first, wrote phonetically "Akwenoy" in his records. "I'll be back in two weeks to check on Akwanoy. Keep the wound clean and watch his pain. Please feed the poor animal. He might like some carrots or apples too, but go lightly with it." The vet shook his head as he walked to the car. Good thing he came to help.

Jenna went back to the horse and stared at him. He blew some air through his nose in a vain attempt at a snort. His eye moved to see her, but he lay there – numb and confused. Didn't Super-Mega-Mart have some horse goods? Jenna seemed to remember a horse section at Super-Mega-Mart. Apples huh? Apples and carrots were pretty cheap. What the hell was she doing? This beast hated her. She valued some small portion of her lost life.

The Indian man smiled a toothless grin and lisped, "Akwënöi mean crazy." Jenna frowned. Yes this was crazy. This animal was crazy. Her mom's hair color was crazy. Mermaid earrings?

The next few days were tiring and somewhat monotonous. Helping the horse seemed to take a good bit of time. The animal was able to stand and just seemed to dazedly eat grass and limp the pasture. The fury was gone, but he still saved up enough energy to eye her with disdain. The Indian man who she realized dated mom had declared that it was actually his name that was Akwënöi, not the horse, but then he laughed and said his name was Chief. Chief went on walks with the horse in which the Indian seemed to have long and drawn out conversations.

Chief said in about three words (he didn't talk much, but when he did it meant something) that they were moving their trailer here to her park to be next to her. Her mother owned a small farm, but Josie wasn't sure what to make of her mother's trailer. A few days ago Jenna would have freaked out. Hell, her mother was an alcoholic of the worst kind. Lately, the amount of things to do and solve and find out had kept her mother down to eight shots of alcohol an evening. Did the Indian man drink at all? He seemed a bit too quiet at times and Jenna had to wonder... did he smoke something? Jenna's mother took her to the side.

She started a cigarette and in a single-handed flourish, handed one to Jenna too. "Moving close to you will be difficult for you I know."

Jenna's mother leaned back and started to explain some things to Jenna about her life. "You have no money. You have a child and a horse. How the hell are you going to get by? How much do you make at Super-Mega-Mart Jenna?"

Jenna wasn't going to tell her mother anything about her income. "I can't remember Mama. But I don't want to discuss money with you. In fact, I'm not sure I want you next door living here. You ain't exactly been the best ma. You're not nice when you drink. You have no faith in me."

Big mama bristled. "My spirit is broke Jenna, I ain't mean no more. Besides, what the hell you gonna do? You can't blame me for everything. I had you when I was 15. It wasn't easy raisin' ya. It was a tough life and you weren't a quiet kid at all. Your daddy passed quickly. I took it out on you too. I'm sorry baby, but I'm always here for you."

"I can hope for good luck. Can hope you stop drinking." Jenna smiled sarcastically.

Jenna had finally bought, with the help of a mute and ponderous Chief, a small truckload of hay, about 10 bags of Horseman's Edge for the future – a pelleted feed, and kept the cookie jar full of those peeled mini-carrots. Feeding time was an entertainment feature in and of itself. It usually subsisted of the family being woken up at 7:30 am to the call of a very grumpy and hungry horse pounding on the ground. "Grumps" as Jenna liked to call him would paw at the fence and bray like an animal in pain and do a dance that none of the neighbors liked. He was now up to a ½ bale of hay, so she would put it over her shoulder and bring it up to him and do her best to not invite his hatred too much as she ran up, shoved the bale over the side and ran back down the hill. Josie found this immensely funny and would often clap to which the horse would lift his head with hay drool spilling out of his mouth and regard Josie with much more respect. Mean horse. Feed him and she still gets no respect. She horse still preferred Josie, though she didn't even feed him.

On Jenna's last shift at Super-Mega-Mart she had bought a cheap nylon halter for the horse that was used supposedly if you want to be in control of your beast. She also bought what was called a lead line – a long line of rope with a snap that you used to hold onto the halter, and then she contemplated a brush – they had a bazillion types of brushes for these animals. Holy cow and hoof conditioners – riding britches, videos... hmmm videos. There were Monty Roberts videos. There were John Lyon's videos. She picked up a free publication called Stablemates – a magazine for the horse industry. It was full of horses for sale and barns and people who thought they could do things with horses. Bingo! This horse industry had some momentum she thought. The brushes were cheap, about a dollar so she bought one. No biggie, and she got her 10% discount too which helped with everything. This time the manager stroked his mustache, adjusted his glasses, and looked on at her purchase.

Jenna apologized to the manager. She felt sorry that Sven had caused so much trouble. So many police and emergencies with this man. She told him how important her job was, how complicated her life was and how much she liked to work.

"Uh, Jenna. You know these horses, they ain't cheap. We heard about the incident by the way." He looked nervous again, like he was reliving the Sven experience in his mind. "I don't know what the hell you did worrying bout' that crazy idiot. I handled him though. He coulda killed ya if I hadn't been there. I feel bad almost taking your job away. You can have your job back. We need you around here."

"Yeah." Chief seemed to have had some sort of effect on her and she kept her conversations short lately. She looked down and the manager regarded her kindly. "Jenna you take another 5% off your order. You need it." Jenna shifted uncomfortably but was happy for the recognition. Usually the manager didn't just give you a discount. Did he want something?

"Get some rest for tomorrow Jenna. Word on the street is we got some secret shoppers tomorrow. Can you show up twenty minutes early to help me with things? I don't think you can sign in on the clock that early, but we could sure use the help and I can let us in early." Super-Mega-Mart used to keep people there all night locked in the store, some only getting three hours of sleep in order to achieve certain standards. It had seemed like a fire hazard and then it had supposedly hit the city papers, and the practice had stopped. As a result, quality had gone down, but the lives of employees had improved significantly. After all, there's more to life than Super-Mega-Mart, right? Probably not when you think about it. Not in this town. Sven had been angry enough to be interesting, and jolt some life caffeine into her blood. But really he was on a one way trip to jail using his angerville pass, and in this world, there are no real "get out of jail free" passes, unless one considered all the free money Sven had gotten out of Jenna for bail money.

Once at home, Jenna picked up the horse magazine and sifted through the ads. She wasn't sure what half of it meant. Josie looked at the mag after Jenna and found she liked the ponies and picked out what was called a strawberry blond Shetland pony and decided she had to have it. Jenna grimaced and shook her head at Josie. "Grumps would kill it. Besides, money-wise we ain't doing so well."

"Grumps isn't bad anymore Jin. I want pony. Grumps is lonely." Josie stated it as if there would be no real argument or discussion about it. The pony was hers, Josie thought.

"I don't know." G Love, now known affectionately as G limped up to the fence and perused the grass near the fence. He pushed his head towards them and a breeze carried through his dirty scraggly mane. The vet bill had been pricey. She didn't need another vet bill.

Mom shifted her weight at the table. She had cooked some rice and beans and the smell of bacon and black beans filled the trailer. "You can't afford another one Jenna. We're helping out though." Though her mother was an alcoholic, she had changed into a nicer one. Her mother was able to stay home and care for Josie. Jenna should have called Child

Protective Services or the police but she worried about Josie and she knew she and her mother cared for the child. They seemed to bond over the child. Because she now hated Sven and she knew her mother hated Sven too, she wanted to protect the child from him. She was worried that if the cops or child protective services became involved, the child would go back to him. She knew he wouldn't care for the child.

Mom was right. She would help by moving closer. Josie was getting the attention she needed and Chief was working with the horse too. And her money, though little, was working to meet needs. They didn't eat a lot but it was getting healthier somehow. No money for McDonald's lately, but it was funny, Josie behaved better when she ate the home cooked foods. They couldn't afford too much meat neither. Mostly rice and beans for lunch and oatmeal for breakfast. A Pop-tart every once in a while ... Jenna knew also that Josie needed to go to school. She had talked to the principal and this was a small town, and he made it sound like they would make it work out. In two weeks the beginning of the school year would start up. Josie would be attending second grade. They would try to test her higher, but start her out in second anyways. She was a little old for second, but that's the way it works when you haven't been in school for a while. Mom thought it was a good start. It's always nice when a family member seems to get better. Mom had been in a daze for a while until now.

Jenna had received a letter from Sven from jail. She hadn't bailed him out this time, likely to his chagrin. The letter read "One down, one to go. Jenna how the fuck could you hurt me like this. Don't you care about my situation? What the hell is wrong with you? I want my fucking $5.00 back." At the advice of Ma and Chief, Jenna showed it to Sheriff Johnson, a short chubby man with a cheek twitch and dark brown hair that parted more sideways than most, who tucked it in his pocket and smiled at her.

"He ain't getting out any time soon. We have suspicions he was involved in another crime.B esides, Lewis is pretty mad about he treated yer family."

She sighed and felt better. She had no idea who Lewis was.

"Who's Lewis?"

Sheriff Johnson's cheek twitched as he smiled a toothy grin. He straightened his shirt. "The Policeman who helped ya."

Jenna remembered the kind policeman. She remembered how he had protected her. She thought he was very handsome but also very kind, deliberate.

Chief had started to halter the angry beast and G seemed like an old pro. So the animated conversation between the Chief and G now involved the halter and lead line. Grumps followed him along and the limp was improving. He just seemed to have a slight limp now. It was more like that leg took just a little more effort. Grumps had started to trot a little bit too. She stopped putting the bute in a handful of grain. And he had gentled a little bit to her feedings. He still made a commotion in the mornings. Now that he felt better, it consisted of lots of prancing and snorting and now, Grumps would actually trot around with the bucket in his mouth. As if to say, ok here it is, feed me! Josie loved it. The claps were excited and happy. Grumps was Josie's constant entertainment.

"I love Grumpies." Josie exclaimed one day. Jenna was not happy with an affectionate term for the beast, but his mortality and suffering had softened her considerably.

Mom laughed over a Coca Cola and the smell of fried potatoes and bacon filled the trailer. Chief smiled and

stretched in his chair. Ma and Chief were not very affectionate. Ma's hair was fading out from that horrifying shade of
fake red. She had cut it short. What had she been thinking.
She had lost the mermaid earrings.

"Mom, your hair looks so much better now."

"Yeah, I know." She laughed and sipped more soft drink.
"I think all that rum and Coke was distorting my viewpoint.
You look better too sweetie. I noticed you ain't smokin' lately.
Some people, they take up food when they don't smoke, but
you somehow let go of both."

The Chief agreed and regarded the horse from inside
the trailer. He spoke today. "In a week, I am going to
ride Akwënöi. He's probably been broke already. Though
I hear that the old boyfriend did not have much sense."
The Chief's English had a slight accent. Jenna wondered
what it was. It sounded a little like those French accents on
television.

Ma regarded Chief and exclaimed, "Well, well. Better
even than watching Jenna feed him. Are you sure it's a
good idea? He still has a little limp. You're not a young man
anymore."

The Chief looked at her dead serious. "And he always
will, but he needs attention, exercise, and the moon says so."
Ma blushed. The Chief's serious look turned to satire and
a long wise smile spread across his face. "In some ways, I'm
still young."

It made Jenna wonder what was so embarrassing about
the moon.

Chapter 3
Horse It Alls

Don't squat on a fire ant pile when you're sizing up your enemy.

— Chief Proverb

Jenna realized that she couldn't take care of Josie and Josie needed more than she could offer her. She also knew it was really over with Sven. She had thought she was helping him again and wondered if he would care more for her if she helped out, but she realized she wasn't sure she wanted to help him anymore. Jenna got in touch with the police and let them know about the little girl she had sort of adopted, and was taking care of. It was Sven's child, that was obvious, but she wasn't sure who the mom was. The police chief said that they would look into it and get the Department of Human Services involved. They gave her the number for the Department of Human Services as well in Atlanta and Social Circle, "in case they take too long. They tend to take a while," the man at the police office told her.

This alarmed Jenna but also somehow made her feel happy. She had to care for Josie.

On a rare occasion when Chief felt like talking, Jenna and Josie were given to listen to him with serious intent to understand. He told them about the danger of "Horse It Alls." Horse It Alls were people given to know everything about horses (a know-it-all, but worse), control freaks bent on controlling the animal and the people around it.

"Six sure signs of a Horse It All." The Chief exclaimed in an assured manner.

"Number one, they will disagree with you to be right, even when they are wrong. Two – they like to yell and pretend to be content and happy. Three – they force their horse into many contraptions. Three they get angry and ride horse into the ground, sometimes literally. Five, inability to be happy with bodily image –"

"Hey!" Jenna exclaimed, looking at herself.

"Lose weight or be happy with your weight. I thought you were happy with weight."

Jenna kept quiet and continued to listen – a little steam dissipating.

"Jen, you are looking and acting better these days. Five, horse not happy. This is a sure sign. Above all else, look at Horse It All's animals. They never happy. They are robots and they are sad creatures who have been forced to lease their souls to this control-nut human. Six, Horse It All not really happy either."

Well, that which Chief had discussed with her was apparently spawned a tangent for his topic of conversation with Josie and G Love (The name G reminded her of the musician G Love and Special Sauce) in the horse pasture. His conversation was particularly animated today and Jenna thought maybe sometime she would go walking with them in the future.

"Hey Jen, how are you?" Ma ambled to her and Jenna noticed Ma had cut the red color almost out of her hair. It had been a cheap color packet and that which was permanent, was almost easily cut out. Her ears were healing from the horrible mermaid earrings. She wore some nice clean cotton clothes made in extra sizes. It was nice to see her in clean clothes. Nice to see her normal. She had only had a little alcohol in over two weeks now.

"You sure G wouldn't like a pony?"

"I don't know Ma. Josie sure would like that, but..." Jenna scrunched up her forehead and thought hard, trying to push away the nightmare of another vet visit. She remembered shelling out the money for the beast.

"She wouldn't be riding that monster at least." G had seemed like much less of a monster lately. His spirit had been dampened by the run in with Sven and his gun. He was more demure about food and more clown than beast. The horse seemed to reward them for treating him kindly. He seemed to be training her. She laughed. She would no longer refer to him as "beast" or "monster" anymore.

"Well, I could call on the strawberry blond pony and see what the owner says. If they've had the horse for a while, they should know something about horses."

"Ma that is totally irresponsible!"

Ma sucked in some air and stared in consternation. "It takes one to know one!"

Jenna and Ma left Josie with Chief and G – and Jenna felt fine about it. There was no wiser and gentler person than Chief. Less than verbal, but his quietude was potent and Jenna respected that. Josie seemed to mature with the Chief with her and she pondered life a little more and learned about the value of thought. She needed more balance, after all life had been very tumultuous before Jenna, Chief and Ma.

Ma had called the lady with the horse. Ma made a lot of grunts on the phone and seemed sold on the pony before she ever got on the phone. Ma got the address and found out that it was about a two hour drive. Did Jenna mind? No, it'd be nice to get away, but should they spend the money?

One exception to Jenna's diet was road trips she decided. She liked Combos and every convenience store had them so she got some Combos, but decided to buy water instead of a Cherry Coke. Ma hovered over the Coke too, but then settled on water as well. "I guess I feel better when I don't drink caffeine and sugah." It was hard to pass up Coca Cola though. Ma chuckled and heaved herself into the car. Jenna wondered if her mother was kicking the habit due to her and their new responsibilities, maybe their relationship was healing.

The car ride was emotionally eventful. Jenna learned quite a bit about Ma and Chief and their relationship, as well as Ma's past. Stuff they'd never talked about before this time.

"So Ma, how did you meet Chief?"

Jenna looked at her mother in question.

"I met him as a teenager when I was young and full of life. Tammy and I used to go to Joe's by the pond over off of Jimmy Carter Boulevard and we'd get a shot of tequila and play some pool. I was desperate for a relationship and here was this quiet older man who used to stare at me. I thought he was really weird and I'd make fun of him. I was skinny back then. He used to sit next to me. He wouldn't say anything for days and he'd obviously been working hard somewhere. He often came in with a sunburn or he seemed to be trying to wind down after a hard day's labor. I started to respect this over time, and I told him one day that I like having him around.

"That was like a spell over him. He never gave up and he talked to me after that. Only a little, but one day he said to me,

'Shirley, I like your aura.' I couldn't stop giggling inwardly. I looked at him with a strong face, not showing my humor at his comment, and he said to me, 'mark my words, I'll hold onto that aura.' I really thought he was weird, but somehow it made me like him more. I had to look up aura in our Webster's dictionary at home. Grandma had gotten mad at me for using that word, she had said it was for people who believed in witches and stuff. Grandma's words actually made me like the Chief more, after all, when you're young, you always like the stuff you're not supposed to, you know. Like your Sven. I mean what the hell were you thinking with that one?"

Jenna looked sideways at Ma. "I don't know. I think that perhaps I had a lot of anger over your alcoholism. It was always a 'I scratch your back, you scratch mine' philosophy with me and I just wanted love. I didn't want to always try to earn something I wasn't sure I'd get from you. Sven liked me and he liked me in an extreme manner – liked me when I was skinny more... He liked me furiously and he was angry about it. And he'd fight for me and keep me safe or so I told myself. I also thought I could change him. He wasn't very faithful and I knew it. He also had to take a lot of medicine for schizophrenia. So maybe I balanced the lack of love with this fierce love that was so extreme and chaotic. So extreme that I guess he was dangerous. It just made me tired when it all came to it though. He stopped liking me so much when I got fat. But he got fat too, and I still liked him, even though he tired me out."

"Did you ever communicate this too him?"

"No, he didn't absorb things, or so I thought. I was always worried he would leave me."

"Sometimes it's best to force that stuff. You know, drive the jerk away so they think it's their decision."

"I have this guarded way of keeping myself from being let go, I have to always let people go first. And I couldn't let go. I've been really messed up."

"Yeah, I can see that. There's strength in not getting caught up in the stupid dating game. In order to find love, sometimes you have to be able to get hurt too. Chief, I knew, would always take care of me. At first, I didn't think him very attractive."

"Really? He seems so emotionally strong."

"He's a tiger in bed."

"Whoa Ma – too much information!"

"Well, no honestly, you have to find someone who worships you – who puts up with you no matter what. Who likes your eccentricities and keeps coming back for more helpings o' you. Yeah when I started drinking, Chief had something to say – he did leave me for a while, but he worried about me and he felt me worthy enough to tell me the truth and make me feel important – and I've always been his center. He calls me his center. I get the feeling he's never liked another woman, like I'm it for him, and if I don't work out, he'll just be alone. I mean how do you top that? Your daddy was ok, but he didn't care about me like Chief."

Jenna looked at the road and saw farmland and an old potted asphalt road that needed repair. "Did he leave just cause you were drinking? And why'd he come back?"

"He left when I started to drink because I tended to run off with random men. I mean I think about how ignorant and easily in love I was and I blush a deep crimson. I hope to god I don't run into people I knew back then. After I stopped the sleeping around part, and after your Bill died, Chief came back a few years ago. He seemed really unhappy. Hasn't said much, but just likes for me to be near I guess."

"Is he my…"

"No no no.." Ma winced. "Bill was your non-biological dad until he died of pancreatic cancer. But, like I told you when you were young – I don't know who your real father was. I didn't bring it up with anyone because I slept and drank and god knows what else. I even did some drugs too. I suspect he was one of my dealers. Jen I was bad. I'm glad you never did drugs. They can affect your whole life. Tamm never left that world. She's in a home now. She OD'd on some LSD. They say the first baby looks just like the dad, but I can't even remember half the people I slept with. Chief accepts that. He says he doesn't care about that stuff. He says his soul knows whether my blood is good with his or not. I say ok. I like his aura too." Ma smiled warmly.

"I'm sorry momma but I did smoke Pot one time with Sven."

"Lord that man is evil. I hope it made you feel like crap. Stay away from that stuff honey. You can do better."

Jenna remembered the one time she had smoked pot. She had woken up with a horrible hangover, more from the tequila than the pot. Her vision had been fuzzy all day and loud noises had hurt her head. She also felt a little depressed that day. She hadn't had a drink since then. She had vowed to herself at that time to never touch drugs again.

"I wonder if you've just had some bad luck with men or maybe you're repeating the past. Bill was ok but when you were young he kind of abandoned us too after your real father abandoned us." She only remembered the older version of Bill with skin yellowed from liver issues, providing advice but not moving around very much.

Even though she had been told this about her father before by her mother, it still hurt her. The emptiness never seemed to go away at times. Maybe that's why she ate so much more these days. The food helped her forget about her bad luck. Jen thought about Josie and how similar their relationship was. Though Josie had a father, he wasn't a father who she could count on either.

Jenna thought of ma when she was young and they talked about the pony. Ma also told Jenna some stuff she'd not heard in a long time.

"Jenna, you're real smart and you can get your GED real quick – you never thought about college? You could run that Super-Mega-Mart, or not care and keep working and wishing you were better. The alcohol and my selfishness really blinded me to your poe-tential. "

Jenna thought about it and started to feel emotional; her eyes misted up with water. Her mother had never been so helpful to her. Her mother had always held her back. Jenna thought the day would never come when her mother tried to motivate her. It gave her some hope but she worried that it may just be a matter of time before her mother started drinking again.

"I've always wanted to learn a language, like Spanish or French." She had learned a little Spanish from the ladies next door when she was a toddler. She still remembered some of it. She thought maybe she was very creative. This change in Ma was amazing. She remembered that the alcohol turned her mean.

"We should have brought Josie!" Ma yelled.

"Oh shit." Jenna looked down at the road. "Are we stupid or what? You sure I can get my GED?" Jenna laughed. She liked sharing the private time with Ma and was glad not to have Josie. She had needed some catharsis. Granted, she now tolerated Josie, but Ma needed to communicate more with her, and this was their bridge.

When they arrived at Meadowbrook Farms the lady from the phone conversation greeted them at the fence with a riding crop in her hand. Her name was Michelle and the pony's name was Buttercup. "We call him Buddy for short." Michelle was tall, about six feet tall with dark blond hair and jodphurs and a monogrammed riding jacket. Michelle talked with a military authoritarian note in her voice, patting her leg with her crop. Buddy was nonchalantly eating grass in the meadow a few yards behind her. Michelle definitely fancied herself an expert. She told Jenna about alfalfa cubes and orchard grass, and special supplements for this and that. She even had vitamin treats she fed to Buddy. Buddy was a very forward pony who had no respect for personal boundaries. He sifted through Ma's pockets and nearly knocked her over looking for treats. At one point when they were getting weary of Michelle's rants, he went between Ma's legs and trotted off with a declarative whinny. It was a nice interruption.

"That's a first." Michelle raised her eyebrows. "He loves kids. He's a special horse. But I've never seen him search through someone's pockets before." Michelle was very serious about everything horse related. She didn't seem to have much of a funny bone.

"Does he like them as much as he likes Ma?" Jenna had made a joke. "How is he with large boy horses?" Jenna thought of G blowing air through his nostrils and charging this little cute pony. "Is he fixed?"

"Oh he loves the boys and the girls. Haven't seen him not get along with anyone. He especially likes the boy horses. Keeps them in line. You'd be surprised what an ordered barn a pony will keep. They're good for keeping order. Yes he is fixed, he's a bit of a mutt. All boy horses should be fixed if they're going to be around other horses."

"We have this huge black horse. He's mean and he likes to threaten us all, but we're afraid this little girl we're taking care of likes the big horse too much and we want something better for a little girl than what we currently have."

Michelle swaggered like a man to show authority. "He's great with everyone. I've been training horses for 20 years now. I know a good pony when I see it. He really connects with your mom and that's no lie. Haven't seen him ever fancy someone so much, in fact. Will probably like the little girl too. Line her pockets with carrots and you'll have a match made in heaven."

A Horse It All. After that the woman feigned extreme happiness and they watched as she rode and was subsequently smooshed (the horse fell onto her, not harmed, she was smiling through it all) by her 16 hand thoroughbred during a riding lesson. Luckily, she walked away from the incident, but it looked like she had literally driven her horse into the ground, by forcing him to try to ride around in circles so tight he just fell forward on two knees and buckled over sideways. The horse, according to her, hadn't been "bending" properly for the student she was teaching. They didn't quite understand it, but the show the woman put on definitely made them think about Buttercup.

"We might want to get Buttercup out of this situation," she mumbled to Ma sideways through her mouth.

"I teach lessons if you want to learn how to ride." Michelle stated it as if it was something that maybe they had already pondered and she was sowing up the odd ends. "Free lesson with Buddy."

"Hmmm. Uh, no thanks. But, onto Buttercup. We can't afford much at all. I noticed Buttercup is $100. I'm not sure we can even afford that." Ma shifted weight to her other hip as she stood in the sun.

Michelle's eyes became narrower. "$100 is the lowest I can go with delivery for $50 extra. Horses aren't cheap. This pony is the best thing for a little girl. He's a little angel and very safe. I've taught this horse some great manners too – You can't beat that!"

Delivery. Good idea.

Ma lifted an eyebrow. "$100 with delivery." Ma grabbed Jenna's arm and they started to walk to the car.

"Ok. um $100 is fine." Michelle yelled after them in a much nicer voice.

Ma pulled out a wad of cash. Michelle had Ma sign some papers and then handed Ma an old bridle for the pony. The pony was sold, "As is. I'd usually love to take my horses back, but I have no more room you see. Cannot take him back." Buddy nudged Ma, almost knocking her over.

"Your big mean horse, is he fixed?" Michelle looked at them inquisitively.

"No, not yet."

"I was told by the last owner that Buddy handles stallions real well. I had an old racehorse they traded me buddy for. I had been thinking about breeding." Michelle shared that she could handle a stallion just fine but that bloodlines were "just everything." And she needed to invest in her training program, not horse breeding.

This made Jenna feel better about everything. A pony for Josie and a horse to calm down the G beast. Jenna would have thanked Michelle, but she was concerned for her horses' welfare given Michelle's show of force.

"I'll deliver him tomorrow." Michelle smacked her riding crop on her leg. Buddy's head shot up, eyeing them all with an air of question. He seemed to think someone had a treat for him.

What had they gotten themselves into?

The next day, Buttercup arrived, much to the dismay of their neighbor who had let the first horse into his field in the first place. He was more like a Butterball than a Buttercup. And when feeding time came, he actually pushed G Love to the side and then tried to steal G Love's food too. G jumped up in the air and almost landed on Buttercup with a hoof neatly placed near the pony's front withers.

It scared the hell out of all of them, because Grumps was furious and chased the pony nearly into the railing several times. He reared and bucked and let the little B know that clearly, he was the boss. As Chief explained one morning over coffee, horses are herd animals and the first herd animal commands respect. If they were to get another pet, G and Butterball would likely be in charge of that horse. Buddy just really liked to test things. One angry furious jump and trot and Buddy realized size does matter. "Best not to interfere. They'll be fine." Apparently, those that overreact often have a few problem horses on their hands – one that never learned to defend itself and another who gets to beat up by other horses without getting it back. With that the pony swiftly kicked the stallion, tapping him with a thump on his right bottom leg. The stallion bit the pony's butt, coming up with a mouthful of fluffy strawberry hair, and the pony kicked again nearly catching the G in the head. A third time and his little misshapen hooves thwacked the stallion in the neck.

"The lady said it'd keep the big one company," Josie told the neighbor who frowned at the little pony as it sifted through his pockets, pushing him. The pony bit his belt buckle and quickly shied when the man flinched at it. Ever the curious animal, the pony continued to sift and finally tried to pull the belt buckle off. The neighbor tousled the pony's light blond forelock and the pony stopped tugging, instead rubbing his whole head into the neighbor, nearly knocking him over. The pony must've had an itch on his head. Long pony hairs were now all over this shirt and jeans. Only a good wash would get all that hair off his jeans.

"I'm happy to see your big horse feeling better." The neighbor noted. "We were really worried about him." The man nodded to his trailer. He was talking about his wife or girlfriend being worried too. He was a real quiet man and they didn't see much of him, and had never seen anyone else around his trailer. She had not noticed anyone else there. He told her she was ill and stayed indoors all the time. She was on oxygen for severe COPD. Too many years of smoking, he said.

He wasn't super happy about the new addition, but little Josie seemed to quell things over for the moment. He looked off into the distance and then put his hand on her head, smiled and pointed at the pony. "You treat this little girl right. And no more horses, little lady." Josie bounced up and down and merrily skipped away to the trailer. "Well, at least I don't have to mow my lawn. I can spend more time taking care of Betty." They heard the man mumble under his breath as he ambled back to his home.

Ma was cooking some rice pilaf and chicken in a mustard sauce. The smell filled the trailer and wafted out over the pasture. Buddy seemed to like the smell and trotted around with his head up in the air, sniffing. G could care less. The grass situation was much more depleted since the addition of Butterball. Jenna consulted with the vet over the phone. He told her to keep the pony on only a little bit of grass and only a tiny bit of grain. "Or he'll founder." the vet told her. Chief had warned her about this too. Founder, huh? There wasn't a lot of grass left in the pasture, so too much grass shouldn't be a problem.

Jenna watched Chief and Josie out in the pasture from her trailer. She had bought a book at Super-Mega-Mart on horse care. Founder was caused by too much protein which cut off circulation to the horse's hooves and caused him to have problems walking. This was a life problem. Once they founder, it affects them for life. Apparently, ponies founder easier than horses

Ma Higgins had given Jenna some additional monies to care for Josie. So she had spent it on a pony and some additional Josie and horse and pony care items. Jenna had also cut back on other expenses to make due. For instance, she no longer purchased hot chocolate on her breaks, finding that free water was far cheaper. She had bought the little munchkin a halter and lead line too, and Jenna found herself worrying when we saw Josie leading the pony around. He was all over the place, sometimes knocking Josie to the ground. Chief would walk G Love with her and Buddy. But Buddy was grabbing grass, he was sifting through her pockets, he was knocking her over, but Chief took the situation and turned it into a good learning experience for Josie. He sternly took both lead lines in his hands and had some words with Buddy who quickly obeyed with head up and a wary eye (of course he had some grass hanging off the right side of his mouth, like he was behaving but he wasn't happy about it at all). He handed Buddy back to Josie who had some stern words with Buddy too. He pushed against her and she pushed back. Buddy shot his head up in the air and eyed her with a distinct disdain (grass still hanging from side of mouth), but then he proceded to behave *a little* better. Josie was learning. Over time he knocked her down less. She looked at the Chief who smiled as she took another yank on the lead line, Josie stuck her chin in the air. No more grass for Buddy while she was walking him! Josie talked to Buddy just like the Chief talked with G Love, except she included stern words and directives.

Before long, Josie was riding the little pony around the pasture with Chief holding the pony with a lead line and she had also started school, so she was bragging to her friends at school about Buddy too. The Chief had had Buddy running around the pasture with feed bags on his back secured on a saddle with hay string for a few weeks beforehand. Buddy at first had tried to buck them off and then Josie (yeah the Horse It All knew everything right? Great horse for kids huh? Maybe you get what you pay for.), but she was a tough little girl and determined to ride him. Buddy was also conveniently low to the ground. An added bonus, Josie lined her pockets with carrots and fed them to Buddy when he was good with her. After months of learning that bucking meant no carrots, the bucking immediately stopped and all thoughts of a cessation of food were impetus for an immediate change in attitude. Buddy also seemed motivated by attention and loved to rub his head on anyone that petted him. You had to be careful with rubbing his itches though because he would often try to knock you over, he would like the itching so much.

"This is a method of testing you." Chief said and lightly thumped Buddy on the head.

Buddy eyed Chief and then tried to rub on Josie. She thumped him on the head and he stood at attention, eyeing her with suspicion. Josie didn't feel bad about it though, after all, he'd nearly knocked her over several times with that rub.

Soon Josie emulated Buddy's behavior and vice versa. Walks were taken with Josie on Buddy's back and the Indian leading the G Love, their wild and mildly tamed pony.

Josie was now the boss of Buddy and not the other way around. Josie was learning to be a leader of the pack. Pack of two, horse and child, but a leader no less.

CHAPTER 4
BLOOD RED NAILS

"There will be a time when you think you're finished. That will be the start of your life."

– *Chief proverb*

After a long day at the Super-Mega-Mart and finally stuck in overtime with the satisfaction of making some extra money, Jenna was happy to be in the safe smell of rotting food and stale cigarettes as she drove her old shuddering and clanky Chevy home on a lonely highway deserted by regular hour workers.

Today at the Mart, Gurdy had talked about the "Union" and passed out informational pamphlets under the doors of the bathroom stalls. Gurdy had worked there for 18 years now without a raise or a promotion. She told them she'd had enough of aisle spills, and managers being promoted because they were men and not women, and she was getting old – word on the street, they wanted to fire her and replace her with someone younger. She said she was caught in the power control of what she called, "the corporate kingdom." Jenna would rather not get stuck in all that. So when a few other employees joined their manager in the back to burn the pamphlets, Jenna thought for job security's sake best to follow suit. She felt a little guilty not supporting Gurdy as she stood there watching her Manager put pamphlets into a metal garbage can. It looked like it was contained which was good. She needed to survive, to care for her new responsibilities and couldn't afford to be a rabble-rouser. She knew it would be wonderful to get more money to survive, but was worried that she would get fired. An old hire, Shannon, who had worked there for four years had yelled at the manager that she was stuck in debt due to her family responsibilities and had demanded a raise. Not only had Shannon been fired, but when she'd applied to work at several other area stores, the word had gotten around that she was greedy. Jenna didn't want to be viewed that way and wasn't quite sure how to climb out of her pay ceiling. Also, she kind of enjoyed the work too.

In short, the bonfire of the 'pro-Union' pamphlets turned out to be a very bad idea. Fires do tend to be unpredictable. Though it appeared safely contained in a garbage can, the wind blew the fire in the exact opposite direction than expected and it caught some boxes on fire and the boxes had some aged lighter fluid containers in them (the manager thought he had asked Jimmy to throw them out into the dumpsters that were to be emptied this morning), which proceeded to blow up. And then, to the dismay of a quivering mustache on the manager, the roof had caught on fire. Instead of calling the police or fire experts he was in response mode. Handlebar mustache man had gathered everyone up, even those complaining about payment, jobs and the building, and herded them to their cars. "Everyone, go home for the day." He had tried to yell into a megaphone under the blaring siren of a deafening fire alarm. Finally, he just ran around, staunch, straight-shouldered with upright and singular determination and told each person he found to "go home now." It was early in the day and not many people were shopping, so it was easy to get everyone out. Gurdy said that there had been a man following her and she thought he was still inside. We laughed as Bob locked up the store – the alarm was on too and had heat sensors – the alarm noted "no movement" before Bob set it. The Fire Department was finally called and he would reset the alarm to let them in once they arrived. Gurdy's gettin' paranoid as she gets older he joked.

Jenna was comfortable in her Chevy's lumpy seat, and thought about all those times Gurdy was right about things like that. 'Maybe there was some union-buster guy stuck in the store' Gurdy had whispered to others. Don't you think a guy like that would have a cell phone? Would a cell phone work in a burning explosive blaze of every cleaning liquid, motor oil, and country rifle bullet known to man? Would a burning Super-Mega-Mart be something akin to a nuclear weapon – I mean think of all that crap mixed together. Burning it could not be a good thing.

She drove along the highway with the radio blaring Beth Orton's, "Oohh girl, things are gonna get easier. Oooh girl, things'll get brighter." She laughed at the song, but then winced, worried. Things were getting easier and brighter and then things would be crappier and darker again soon. She felt comforted by Beth's smooth assuring voice. She just needed one cigarette. She pulled out a cigarette and enjoyed it thoroughly. Every once in a while would be ok, right? She just wasn't a cold turkey quitter.

When Jenna got home to tell the Super-Mega-Mart soap opera news to Ma, she noted a sickening smell emanating from the trailer. It was the stench of throw-up, cigarettes and Coca Cola that had sat out too long and maybe eaten its way through a paper cup. She noticed the paper cup on the stained linoleum floor and how it sagged and bulged at the sides next to Ma who was face up on the floor, like a lonely human island in a sea of waste. Throw up was just to her right. And Josie started to pound on the bedroom door as soon as she realized Jenna was home – the banging echoed on the trailer's flimsy frame. The Chief was not around. Josie must not have gone to school today. Ma had not gotten her off to school yesterday either. All this unpaid overtime had gotten in the way. She should have called the police or child protective services for the child.

"Josie hold on dear. Uh – MA?" Jenn bent down and shook her to see if she was doing alright.

Ma belched in her sleep. She had applied nail polish to her nails incorrectly and her hand was slathered in a sick red that was imperfect and grainy, and not on her nails. The kitchen sink was filled with splatters of red hair dye that had never made it to Ma's hair or down the drain.

What a fucking day after all. She had thought things would get better. Somehow Super-Mega-Mart going up in flames had seemed like a good thing at first. Of course it wasn't, no matter what Gurdy said. Bad things, even happening to "the corporate kingdom" Gurdy spoke of, was not a good thing, because no matter what, good people worked there. And good people needed an income, and Super-Mega-Mart brought them an income.

Jenna needed a time-out for her life. Like she was in a movie and at this point, could say "ok, cut!" and everything would stop and she could get a nap in. Holy shit. Do all folks have this much drama? Could someone possibly BE this unlucky?

"Ma, what happened?" This seemed a rhetorical question since Ma had now passed out cold. Whimpering came from the bedroom. Jenna felt stuck. She felt a deep sense of disappointment about her mother and she felt like her life was on the "repeat" button again. She remembered the countless other times she had found her mother like this. She felt like the bonding moments she had had with her mother were deceiving, when Ma had helped her get the pony. She knew her mother couldn't stay sober and Jenna had enough of her own problems. Having her mother drunk again just complicated her life way worse than she needed. Especially today of all days. But Jenna thought, 'she is still my mother.' A big weight seemed to sit on Jenna's chest. She went to the bedroom door and opened it. Josie had tear-streaked cheeks and her little eyes were puffy. Jenna held her close and rubbed her little back.

"It's ok baby. Ma just overdid some drinking. She'll be ok. Don't drink when you get older, k?"

Josie nodded fervently, staring at Ma's open mouth and sickly pallor. Ma Higgins did not look good. She looked very sick.

She wished someone was there to help her with Josie. She hated Josie seeing her Ma like this. She wanted to take Ma to her car to get her to the hospital, but she was so heavy. She attempted to drag her, but it made things worse, taking the rug and the table with her. Ma made a moaning noise. Jenna relaxed a little. A moaning noise couldn't be bad. Another belch came and ma started to choke and sputter and spasm. Jenna tightened again. Josie wiped her face with her hands as tears came again. Maybe she was throwing up?

Jenna, with all effort possible, rolled ma on her side. She felt all the lack of muscle in her arms and the effort tired Jenna considerably. What a stink came from Ma's mouth! Jenna tried not to smell it, but the full force of Ma's uncleanly stink hit her like a skybound train into both nostrils. Jenna heaved a little, but thankfully, did not add to the mess. Throw-up piled out of her Ma's mouth and heaped into a liquid mess on the floor. Ma coughed in her sleep and more throwed up oozed out. A sick red slathered hand came to her mouth and Ma suddenly came to, sick and numb and a ghastly shade of green and red. She had been smoking too, a sick smell of gingivitis, stomach acid, drink, and cigarettes filled the trailer with it's liver cell-killing omens.

"Sorry, Jin. So sorry." Ma's voice was gritty and slathered in throw-up chunks, like a woman who ate three times her size, smoked too many cigarettes, and spoke through it all. Jen saw empty liquor bottle in her ma's purse. So she had snuck some in in her purse from her trailer? Jenna did not keep alcohol in her trailer so she had not expected this. But her mama's trailer wasn't far. She thought all the liquor had been removed from her mama's trailer.

Jenna helped her to bed, almost getting crushed, then almost broke a few pieces of furniture, but finally making it to the bedroom with Ma's burdened help as Ma helped to walk on her unsteady legs. After getting there and laying down, Ma started to snore something awful.

Jen and Josie found all the alcohol that it was possible to find, all the cigarettes they could and threw it all into a large garbage bag, readying the mess for the garbage men. They tried, but couldn't get all the red nail polish off the sofa. Ma could still be a pain.

"I don't like red. Red means your Ma is drinking." Josie frowned. Her eyes were big, concerned-like and she told Jen in one breath, "Chief and Ma got in fight about something in her purse and ma locked me in the bedroom and they left. Ma came back and I heard her say bad words, and then I heard her open a bottle." Josie was talking in more complete sentences.

Jenna hugged her. "It's ok now, baby." She felt Josie's soft silky ringlets and tried to comfort her sad eyes with a long-lasting hold.

A loud sputtering and banging came from the bedroom. A lamp or something fell and broke, the sound of shattered glass through a paper-thin particle-board door with oak veneer glued onto it.

"Ma?" Jenna yelled into the small space. She leaped to the door and shoved it open. Ma was a greenish blue palor and Jenna quickly rolled her sideways again. A drool mixed with throwup rivered out of her mouth and soaked the thin cotton sheet.

"Jin, my head hurts like a car just ran it over. This is worst than my worse hangovuhhh." Her speech was slurred. Her body was twitching.

"Ma, hospital hurts, or rest hurts?"

"I might should hospeetaaaal." She spat the eetaal part of hospital like breathing hurt. One side of her face didn't look right, her right nostril and lip lower than her left ones.

They helped a swaying and sweating Ma into her old Chevy, clearing away the debree, and then shoving Ma into the backseat with the best help possible given the situation, sprawled across People magazines and Oreo wrappers, like a large whale among the little fish that got her there in the first place. The car heaved and sunk as Ma hit the seats. Ma was having difficulty walking and talking. Josie tried to get in the back with Ma, a protective hand on Ma's foot.

"Jin, I sit back here with Ma." She was a mess. Her shirt was dirty, she smelled like hay, and her hair was dishevelled and some of it sticking to her face.

"Sit with me in the front, sweetie." Jenna softened and put a hand on her shoulder. "Ma ain't feeling so well, and I don't want her throwin up on ya." She also didn't want the thrashing to commence and get Josie hurt too, but didn't want to worry Josie.

Ma shivered and wretched a few times on the way, her color returning a little and then fading again. When they arrived at the hospital, it was full to the brim in emergency. Other folks looked just as bad off as Ma, one guy with a nail through his arm, obviously in great amounts of pain. American healthcare used to be so good, Jenna remembered. She remembered when the hospital gave her eye surgery when she was 8 or 9 years old and went to every effort to make it smooth, giving her extra pain meds (which she didn't need afterall), and she got an IV after they numbed up her arm. These days you have something going in, and it's just as likely you'll get something going out. She'd read about a special type of flesh-eating bacteria, MRSA, running rampant in American hospitals. She shuddered a little and tried not to think about it. She felt bad for AIDS patients whose immune systems might not be able to handle these things you pick up just before you leave the hospital. Her friend Vicky had worked as a CNA before Super-Mega-Mart and the hospital staff told her they'd have a flesh-eating bacteria patient in one room and transfer him to another room, which meant the next person in his old room might get it too. Scary!

They brought Ma up to the counter. The woman at the counter noted her color and apologized outright. "We're a bit understaffed at the moment, I'm so sorry for the wait."

An ill melodious symphony of pain started. Ma started to choke and fell to the floor. One side of her face looked off kilter again. Her poorly painted nails scratched the wall and some cheap red polish smeared on the wall like a crayon streak. Jenna suddenly felt like she was in a horror movie. The man with the nail in his arm started to shake a little and had turned a marble white. Ma was writhing on the floor, people in the waiting room were watching in terror as Ma preceded to contort on one side of her body. The woman behind the counter gulped and called a special code on the intercom. Two men and one tall woman ran to Ma's side from large blue-green hospital doors. They leaned over her and forcefully put her sideways. They hovered enough that Jenna felt like she was in the way.

"Why is her face all weird? Holy Sh –" Was all Jenna could say as she nicely pulled Josie back with her while the team worked to get Ma better. She hoped Josie hadn't heard the word, but it was what this situation warranted. She tried to turn Josie away, but Josie's attention was glued. Sometimes the honesty and desperation of this world was what had to be. She wanted to shield her from this life and it's sometimes harsh reality. Poor Josie. Jenna had doubts about involving Josie in all of this, but it was too late anyway.

A large bed was wheeled in and a board had been put under Ma. The board was heaved onto the bed and she was wheeled away. Medical people hovered around her working at the board moved. The man with the nail in his arm was also called and taken back through the great big hospital doors. Men and women with outfits in shades of blue, shethoscopes and serious expressions milled about in the background. Jenna started to bite her nails and let Josie sit on her lap. "It's ok baby." She said to Josie as much as she said it to herself. Yeah she was mad at her ma for all the drinkin', all the hatred and meanness and independence, but hell, she loved the woman. The woman was blood, kin, someone to sort of rely on. Another person in the world who she knew and cared for. Ma had started to get better, but then the wagon came along and Ma had jumped off it. Though Jenna found herself deeply disappointed, she also remembered the kindnesses of her mother, her sober times. The good work that her mother had done for community before she became overwhelmed by it all.

A tall woman with dark short hair and a stethoscope around her neck bust through the doors and walked towards Jenna and Josie as the desk lady pointed her their way. "Are you related to Vera Higgins?" She had clear skin with freckles on her face, a hawkish nose, and dark eyes that pierced them through her glasses. She leaned over and regarded them with a detailed curiosity that took Jenna back.

"Yes, ma'am." Jenna was nervous wanting to respect this woman who clearly in charge. Josie shifted.

"Can I talk to you in private?" The woman eyed the girl, but gave a crisp smile, bordering on concerned as the smile seemed practiced. Jenna had no one to give Josie to. She worried about Josie being involved in all this. She sensed Jenna's inability to leave Josie in the lobby. "I am an Acute Care Nurse Practitioner here in the ER. Follow me."

"Sure, but the kid has to come too." Jenna picked up Josie as she stood up. Josie was a heavy forty pounds. Jenna groaned a little and then gently put Josie next to her standing, and led her along with the lady who seemed to have something to tell them. Hopefully it was good news. Ma had improved along the car ride. Josie stuck to Jenna like a rubbery glue, almost stepping on her feet as they walked. Josie was getting taller and heavy.

They sat in a small medium blue and turquoise room that smelled like baby powder and Clorox. There were vinyl chairs and medical tables with telephones. A television sat in the corner. The woman's stare intensified. She sat across them silent and still, sizing Jenna up. A slight frown at Josie.

"Ms. Higgins?"

Jenna nodded.

The lady had her hand on Jenna's knee. "Well, Ms. Higgins, your mother didn't make it. It was, it was a quick ending, and we gave her enough medication to ease her pain. We gave her medication to thin her blood as soon as we got the IV in, but she had what we call a massive Cerebral Vascular Accident, a stroke, likely earlier today. We tried everything, but she had the stroke and she was in bad shape. We know she had a history of transient ischemic attacks too, this increases her risk of stroke. She also had a family history of stroke. We thought it we gave her medication we could get some more brain function, halt the progress of the stroke. The stroke affected the whole side of her body and ultimately her brain too."

Jenna swallowed, possibly some air got gulped down out of fear and nervousness.

"Uh, ok." She was stunned and any words she said wouldn't make sense. Best to be agreeable. She always had a delayed reaction to bad news. Josie didn't cry audibly, but tears rolled down her cheeks like tiny rivulets. She held onto Jenna with a death-grip that told Jenna not to let her go. Jenna didn't want to break down in front of Josie. She did her best to remain strong. She had just started to become so close to her mother and had found some healing and solace in her relationship with Ma Higgins.

"That was so quick. Was there anything I could have done sooner to save her?" Said Jenna looking questioningly at the Nurse Practitioner.

"I'm so sorry. We tried all we could to save her. My team did CPR as long as possible. We gave her medication to try to address her health. We did our best." The woman now looked at Josie too, concerned.

"I still don't understand." Jenna said weakly.

"It's hard to understand these things when they happen so quickly. She was quite young." Said the woman. "It sounds like she had been drinking for a while. I don't know that you could have done anything." The woman paused, looking at Jenna with serious concern. "How are you handling all of this?" The woman addressed Josie. "Sometimes this news is hardest on the grandchildren."

"She's not my grandma, but she has been nicer than most people." Josie mumbled, not making eye contact.

The woman frowned but her beeper went off. She read it and appeared to think for a second. "Unfortunately, I ha-have to go help someone else. I wish I could stay longer and talk more with you." The look of Jenna gave the woman a short stutter but she collected herself quickly. Jenna was white like a bleached sheet.

"Thank you for letting us know and doing what you could to try to save her." Jenna looked to her lap.

The lady crossed her arms. She seemed ready to handle any situation. "Certainly." She remained poised, professional, affected but stoic. Jenna was reminded of the character Keanu Reeves played in the Matrix. This was his female equivalent – staunch, objective, straight-forward. Getting her job done and reliable. Jenna could see the tell-tale signs of hard work though. A bead of sweat was on the top of the woman's neck near her hairline. Make-up lines on her jaw, hinted to Jenna that her makeup had been hastily applied. Eyes were slightly blood shot possible from working a long shift. But the woman's hands and nails were clean and her strength reassuring to Jenna. But Jenna felt lost too. Where was her Ma? Did she go to heaven? Was there a heaven?

"We also have a 1-800 number if you need to talk to someone about your loss." The lady handed her a pamphlet with the hospitals logo on it and an image of a woman crying while on the phone. Jenna imagined a woman in India, underpaid by an international calling company, helping her deal with her grief, while the underpaid third-world woman listening probably had enough of her own problems. She felt guilty about doling out her problems to others. No way would she call a stranger to discuss her problems.

Jenna worked things out at the desk and left the bright lights of the hospital with its overcrowded and moaning emergency room, its smell of cleaning products in excess, it's green and blue relaxing hues of paradoxicity and blare of shouts and lights and important people carrying instruments with them as they sauntered about. With the white lab coats enveloping a purposeful body, determination singing through linoleum corridors, like an opera of appliances that are actually people humming in a strange and melodious clean medical chorus.

At home things were quiet. The trailer brought back bad memories. It stank like a cheap evening of ill repute with Sven. Josie got some paper towels and started to clean the floor. She was quiet and sniffling. Tears fell onto the paper towel. Jenna felt like a robot, emotions bottled up and caught at a dam; to tired to recognize or accept any sadness. She wiped Josie's beautiful cocoa face with a papertowel. They got what they could off the bed and then covered it with a bedspread then an old sheet and fell asleep, Josie sucked her thumb, and they cuddled together in sleepful purpose, hoping to erase this night's bad events. No amount of warmth or coolness would wake them until morning. They were exhausted.

Jenna lit some candles to try to replace the smell but blew them out later to prevent a trailer fire.

Morning brought no more good omens. Chief showed up and looked almost as bad as Ma had. This gave Jenna and Josie a bit of a sniffle. Both were quiet, out of grief. Jenna had been on the phone with funeral parlors and the like all morning. They would have to cremate her and put her remains in an urn. It's all they could afford.

"Chief, Ma is dead." Josie ran to the bedroom and slammed the door. Sobbing could be heard. The Chief darkened in color and ran a hand across his forehead. His large eyes filled with feelings and he looked through Jenna, into the past.

"Then, I must go. I find little light left in this world without her aura, but I'll find peace." Jenna couldn't react. His words seemed cheesy to her and she felt guilty for thinking such a thing. She nodded. The nod felt like slow-motion. Chief left, quietly, disappearing out of reality, walking through the day breeze on his walk to the highway. He had a cane with him that he leaned on. G Love neighed and danced at the Chief's figure, which he saw along the road as he became smaller and smaller, his figure zig-zagging in the perversion of the heat that surrounded him.

Jenna went into a rage and slammed a chair against the wall. She broke a lamp and threw some bottles to the floor liking the crunch of the glass. For a lifetime she had kept her thoughts about her mother bottled up inside her. And then when she had dared to get closer to her mother, to establish a healthy relationship, her mother had gone over the edge and died on her. She filled a small glass with some bourbon that had been left by her mother under the bed but couldn't drink it. She slammed that too to the floor. Then she felt selfish. She was still alive. Why was she mad at her mother for doing what she had done all her life?

Josie cracked open the door timidly, scared. Jenna did her best to pull herself together.

"I'm so sorry Josie. I'm mad, but I'm never mad at you honey, ok?"

Josie's eyes went wide, concerned. "ok." She said. She slowly came into the room and hugged Jenna warily.

They got a large tin tub and filled it with detergent and the sheets. They rubbed the sheets against a washboard and then hung them up on lines of string in the backyard. Wet, clean smelling sheets flapped in the breeze. Chief was gone. They were sober, but things would improve. Jenna was optimistic because she had always persisted, always survived somehow. Time was her weapon against misfortune. Each day seemed to be a new day for Jenna despite misfortune. Jenna's eyes damned up with salty fluid and she wiped her tears away quickly, hiding her emotional state from Josie. She would cry more tonight in private, she would rage more in private if need be when Josie wouldn't hear her. They needed to be strong. They went around to the front where Butterball and G Love nibbled the grass in content. She was relieved that G Love and Buttercup had worked out their differences. Buttercup was almost underneath the larger horse. Josie and Jenna grabbed some bails of hay and threw them into the field. Butterball and G Love grabbed the hay from all sides and pulled it apart in sudden anticipation of eating it. Buttercup rolled in a patch of it and then the stallion nickered and nuzzled Buttercup out of the way. Suddenly the larger horse mounted the smaller one and this gave Jenna a scare as she reacted suddenly by grabbing Josie, turning her the other way and covering her eyes. Akwenoi's large manly tool slathered Buttercup's hind end, as Buttercup stood on hind legs and peed onto the ground. Josie could see none of this thankfully as Jenna shielded her from seeing it.

"Oh good lord!" Jenna laughed nervously and then tears fell for another reason, still covering her little Josie's eyes. "G Love is REALLY confused! Butterball is a boy." Her welling of emotion led to lots of laughs and so many tears she had to wipe her face with her shirt as she and Josie headed back to the trailer. She couldn't stop laughing and wondered if the emotions from past days had now turned to a welling of laughter as she felt she might cry too. Josie didn't understand these mixed emotions, but just held onto her hand and followed, walking next to her. A little girl who needed other children – this life was getting a bit too serious for the little one, Jenna thought.

Ma Higgins had funeral directions in a small diary at her home. Her mother had expressly asked that she be cremated and only a very small ceremony take place at Jenna's home. Ma Higgins didn't want fanfare. She also noted "please don't tell anyone I died, unless they ask, ok?" This was written in the footnotes. Jenna had planned to have a small private ceremony with Josie at home. Jenna realized she didn't know any of her mother's friends anyways, who would she invite anyways? They had no known further family. There was a cantankerous Louisiana group of Higginses but they were known for their eccentric qualities and spent more time judging her mother than helping her. Claudette Higgins was the matriarch and had long ago outcast her mother due to "definite immoral leanings." Claudette was very focused on the moralities of life and lost focus on her own life by judging others. She starched her dresses, kept her home so sparkling you could run a finger along a counter and never encounter dust. Unbeknownst to the rest of the family, Claudette suffered from obsessive personality disorder and ultimately was hit by a car while trying to tell it to slow down. She had posted 'slow down!' signs in her neighborhood, but her street was a side street for a much busier street. The signs had gotten bigger and bigger until Claudette herself had decided to go into the road 'and stop them myself.' The driver was an out of town New Yorker, lost on the side street but suddenly realizing where the street led to, not noticing Claudette between his map and his car's speed. That was many years ago, but Jenna had never forgotten the printout in the town paper of the crime scene. Her Aunt had sent it to her, but then her Aunt had died of a stroke shortly after that. Uncle Skipper was in Mexico enjoying his new hips but she had no address for him. She could imagine him dancing to a Mariachi band. He used to love to dance, anywhere or anytime. Skipper was also very judgmental of her mother and she didn't feel he would have kind words for her or for Ma. She didn't know anything about any further family.

That evening, she and Josie lit all the candles they could find and found an old Bible Jenna had accidentally kept from a trip many years ago. Jenna had picked up what she thought was her library book, but instead she had picked up the Bible. She had felt guilty about the possibility of throwing out a Bible so she had held onto it. The library book she paid for losing.

She and Josie had cleaned up the trailer. Josie had collected wildflowers and made a ring of wildflowers that they placed around her mama's picture. They did not yet have her cremated remains. According to the morgue, cremation would take approximately two weeks, possibly more. They couldn't afford to expedite anything. There was an extra charge if you needed it quickly.

They sat and looked at the picture. Josie and Jenna cried and talked about their recent good experiences with her mother. Her sobriety brought out Vera's helpful qualities and she had remembered the good times with her mother before she had turned to alcohol.

She told Josie about the time her mother had rescued her from an 8th grade party. When Josie had gotten there she'd noticed a lot of older people at the party and was really confused. Apparently, the 8th grader who had invited her had an older brother in college. The older brother had driven into town with several friends and had their own party too, they were mostly drunk. Being young boys and inebriated at that, they realized that some of the eight graders were pretty. Josie had called her mom from a hall phone. One of the boys had a BB gun and was shooting it at the behind of one of the girls who wore braces.

"Momma, things are kind of weird here." Her mamma was on alert because these were also the children of Bart and Nancy. Bart was a lawyer and had been in her mamma's treatment center several times for cocaine and alcohol. She couldn't tell Jenna this because she had to respect his right to privacy but Vera had worried that his children might also be irresponsible.

Vera was there in five minutes with four policeman. The party stopped and everyone had to go home. Part of Jenna was very embarrassed that her mom had shut down the party but she also knew she was in over her head and wanted to protect the girl with braces. What if they aimed the BB gun at her head? The girl with braces had hugged Jenna the next day, fervently happy for a new friend.

"She was kind of a like a grandmother when she didn't rehydrate." Said Josie, smiling through her tears. "Whatever she drank smelled bad too."

"Yes, she was mostly nice when she was herself." Jenna smiled to Josie.

One large candle stood next to Ma Higgins picture, it was not yet lit.

"What do we read from this?" Josie gestured to the Bible.

"I have no idea, little one." Jenna was kind of apoplexed as to what to say. "Should we just open it and read something?" Jenna worried it would be judgmental nonsense like Claudette spewed out.

They opened the Bible. She opened it to the verse of Matthew which read "Blessed are those who mourn, for they will be comforted." Jenna promptly closed the Bible and felt a sense of relief but bewilderment. She wondered at the luck of finding such a verse, but then realized there was a bookmark there. The bookmark said "Bill and Jo's Candies." It had chocolates and cherries all over it. A flower petal was in the page too. A red rose petal.

Josie lit the candle, smiling at Jenna. A tear ran down Josie's cheek. "I loved Ms. Higgins more than chocolate and I love chocolate."

They closed their eyes and sat together. The candle danced, making shadows in the trailer. The smell of the candle and wildflowers filled the trailer.

Now, who would watch Josie? Would they again take Josie back to school without problems? She had missed a week of school. That was selfish of me, Jenna thought. I need to make sure she doesn't miss school. Maybe school had an afterschool program? She probably couldn't afford it.

Jenna thumbed through her address book. Shit. She really had gotten lazy. Lately, she didn't have time to be lazy with all that was happening. She thought of Candy but realized Candy reminded her of her mother when drunk. Where were all the friends she used to have? Most of them had mutual aholisms – cigarette-aholism, alca-holism…etc…not so healthy of a friendship, but nonetheless, some sort of connection with another person. Didn't she need a job too? She remembered the roof catching on fire at Super-Mega-Mart, the explosion, and Gurdy acting all weird. Had there really been a guy following Gurdy? Was there some dead guy in the Super-Mega-Mart? Oh jeez. What to do … Maybe she could take Ma's job at the quickie-mart? Yuck. Not safe neither when you thought about it. She had a newspaper from last week stuffed somewhere. She found it and started reading the classifieds. Maybe watch kids at her house? What would they think of the big crazy horse? Hmmm….The local community college was looking for an assistant. Tuition discount included. GED required. What the heck was she thinking? She didn't even have her GED yet!

Why the heck not? She could at least try. She remembered Ma's words. "You're real smart Jenna, you can git your GED." Super-Mega-Mart had kindly offered her financial assistance and pay due to displacement by the fire which she had accepted. Another Super-Mega-Mart (the closest one, twenty miles away) offered her employment as well, but she was worried the Chevy could not handle such a drive regularly and didn't want to commit to something she could not follow through on.

Two hours later, Jenna and Josie walked up to the counter at Social Circle Community College. She loved the name of the town.

"Hi, I'm here about the assistant job you have advertised." Jenna was dressed neatly in something she had cleaned a few days ago. She smelt of clean grass. It was a polo shirt and plain dark blue khakis with only one hole near the bottom of them. Her hair was pulled back. Josie was cleaned up and her hair was pulled back too. She sucked her thumb and leaned on Jenna. It reminded Jenna to try her best to find Josie some friends. Jenna was starting to be Josie's only salvation.

"Oh yes, hi. I am Keesha." The jolly African-American woman jiggled behind the glass at the counter and smiled and looked at Jenna, then reminded internally of work, turned to papers and nodded. Then the woman noticed Josie who looked so different than Jenna. She looked from Josie to Jenna. "Please fill this out and Ms. Jojo'll meet with you." She giggled and pointed at Josie who hid behind Jenna's legs. "Hey you lil cutie." The woman's fingernails were long, fake and red with small art on them. Her makeup was caked on like Leonardo Davinci's painter's palette, thick, but colorful. "She can stay with me while you meet with Ms. Jojo." The lady smiled a bright big smile, a gap showing between the teeth. "I'm Keesha, deary. I will make sure you are happy while your mom meets with the nice lady. Do you like coloring books and stickers?" Josie peeked around a leg. Jenna sighed, relieved. This lady was very kind, and this seemed like a nice place. Jenna trembled in fear. Her like of this place made her nervous. Keesha brought around some crayons and a piece of notebook paper as well as some stickers. She eyed Jenna's application. Jenna had noted Gurdy as a reference, as well as her neighbor, and the teenager that she had cleaned up all the spills for. She had started to write her Ma's number, but started to tear up and didn't want to make a scene, so she toughened back up real quick.

"I have my little girl Zeena in daycare here. We receive discounts on daycare. This is the best place to work. I couldn't recommend it more."

"Oh, wow. I hope I get the job." Jenna was scared.

"Girlllllll, you do not have anything to be nervous bout. School's out for summer and everyone's left and we need a stellar assistant. We were about to hire old Tweena, but she can't read very well. She has those cataracts you know and well, Barnhart's been keeping her busy since their marriage. Hmmm hmm."

Jenna tried to smile but her teeth were dry and her lips stuck to them. Josie hummed as she pointed to a very scribbled version of Buttercup on the paper. "Buttercup."

"Who is Buttercup, and who named her Buttercup? Isn't that a movie name?" The lady giggled and looked at Josie.

"Oh, Buttercup is her pony." Jenna let out a nervous laugh. "Not a child's name at all." She felt better and laughed a little better.

"I was going to have to talk to the lady that named poor Buttercup. But it does sound like a pony's name." Keesha put her hands on her thighs and then sat back down behind the counter. Her bright red lipstick shimmered under the lights.

Jenna met with Jojo Patel, the head of the administrative department. She was a petite Indian woman with a very slight accent and a very delicate way about her. She smelled of sandalwood and baby powder. She told Jenna she didn't need references and offered her the job right away. There was one catch – she would have to get her GED within six months of hire.

"I like to give people a chance, but legally you should have your GED to work here. I know you can do it, Jenna. Otherwise, if you don't think you can, I have to hire someone else."

Jenna had looked at her seriously and nodded. "I'm sorry I'm so nervous, but yes, I absolutely want to get my GED ma'am." Jenna's legs crossed, then uncrossed and she fidgeted. Her teeth still felt dry.

Jojo looked over her bifocals. "No worries, dear. I trust you. You can relax."

Jojo had told her that there was a trial period of 30 days in which they could fire her if she didn't perform and in which she would not have healthcare. She could use the childcare, but it would cost full-price until the 30 days was up, but was relatively affordable at baseline. They didn't need her on weekends. Just full-time during the week. She would start tomorrow if that's ok?

Josie needed to be in school anyways. Oh hell, Jenna had forgotten about school already. She hoped things would get better. She hoped she could be a mama for a little while. What would she do with Josie anyways? This was the country, and there weren't places for kids with no mamas out in the country. Where was her mama anyways? Jenna had started to worry of late that now that she was getting attached to Josie, and vice versa, someone would come to take Josie away. The town knew about Sven, and so they protected the girls in that way, but there must be some black woman out there missing her daughter. Hadn't Josie said her momma died? Jenna tried to push it away, but it nagged at her depths, and she knew in her soul that something must be done. Some attempts must be made.

Jenna started her job and sent Josie along each morning to school. A rickety old bus that smelled of old fuel would pick Josie up, pigtails and all, and then when Josie was done at 2:30pm it would drop her off at the community college and then Josie would be in daycare for two hours and they would drive home together. Jenna made fast friends with Keesha who absolutely adored the pair. Zeena and Josie hit it off well too, having draw-offs in which they would try to outdo each other with horrible horrible drawings that they both thought were the best ever. And Jenna and Keesha would coo over them. Zeena did have a habit of picking on Josie, but Josie had started to stand up for herself, thank goodness.

Two months later (Jenna had passed her GED already), Keesha brought up the inevitable. "Girl, you should adopt Josie or figure out who her mother is." Jenna stared at her computer. She googled "adoption." One hundred thirty five million results. Holy friggin' cow!

"Yep. Dad is a no-good and in jail though. I don't want him hurting Josie or knowing about her. Have you seen Sven Stevenson on the news? He has some anger management issues. Josie told me a while back that her mother is dead, though I'm not sure she understands the concept." Jenna realized her vocabulary was improving. She was trying to appear up to her job and more organized. As a result, she was feeling more organized, Jenna version 2.0.

"Yeah."

"Sven is the child's father, Keesha. He is very bad news." Jenna swiveled her chair around.

"Goodness. You should wait a while. Maybe he will self-combust or something. Men with anger give themselves bad luck. Wait, I heard something on the news about him. Something about him and a lady-I think he is in jail Jenna. Those crazy men and their ladies." Keesha laughed but caught herself concerned as her bosom shook the desk.

Jenna laughed too warily. She wondered what kind of lady. She didn't really want to know.

Keesha was lucky. Her husband was a professor at the college and when he stopped by, he was all eyes for Keesha. He bragged about her to Jenna and brought Keesha sweets and snacks. He loved her with food, but loved her all the same. Keesha felt the same about him, showering him with a variety of cute and sophisticated pet names that made Jenna giggle and blush. Keesha gave her hope that maybe, just maybe, there was more to men than just Sven's lack of capabilities.

One time, Professor Ralph Wiggins had brought Keesha some chocolate covered cherries he had bought overseas. "Now Jenna, I know you want some." Wiggins eyed her with a certain flair of amusement and suspicion as he passed them under her nose. "But, these are for my girl, you hear? Ahh, ah, don't you take one. They have roses and saffron in them too. Imported from India, only the best will do for Keesha."

Keesha had shown up right then.

"What are you doing wafting my gifts for others?" Keesha looked at Jenna, laughed and pulled the sweets over to her. She opened it and grinned from ear to ear.

"Dearest, you have outdone yourself yet again. These cherries smell like roses and something else too ... saffron? They smell so good, so creative!"

"Anything for you Keesha. I know what you like." Wiggins leaned into Keesha and he gently massaged her shoulder. It didn't seem lewd, but seemed caring and soulful. Keesha laughed and leaned into him. They both smiled into each other's eyes and found contentedness there.

Later Keesha and Jenna ate the cherries together. "There is absolutely no way I can finish these on my own. It's the thought that matters. If I ate everything he brought me, I would get very fat. No, I share everything. Makes me popular too. Who doesn't love chocolate?"

Jenna tasted very complex flavors. She had never tasted cherries and chocolate like this.

Keesha asked, "Jojo tells me you are taking a language class, no?" Keesha said the 'no' part with a little bit of a French accent.

Jenna nodded. The campus was now busy with the start of fall classes. She had decided to take a Spanish class this fall. She received 50% off tuition and a grant based on her low-income. It was so affordable, she barely had to pay for it.

Chapter 5
Lewis

In order to know how to have good judgment, you had to make a whole lot of bad decisions that helped you learn what it meant.

– Chief Proverb

A cop showing up at your work is usually not a good thing. I mean it's nothing you ask for. When you're home at night asking your creator to watch over your loved ones, you don't add at the end, "oh yes, and please have a cop show up at my work, so that everyone can look at me strangely and think I'm up to no good."

"Good morning ladies." A tall man of six foot four sat behind Keesha's counter. Keesha knew him from church. She smiled largely revealing perfect teeth that appeared to glow in the light. She wore a well-starched pink top and some black trousers. Around her neck, she donned an ornate wooden necklace with carved beads that her husband had bought her some years ago. He had told her it was for his African queen. Her skin shimmered in the flourescent lighting. Maybe her ancestors in Africa were royalty. She sure felt like it.

"Lewis! How's class going? Are you part of my fan club? Did you bring me any sweets?" Keesha put a file in her stack of things to do and donned eyes at the policeman.

"Not bad Ma'am. No sweets, no. Just working my hardest to get an A to stay in good with the Sheriff." He took off his hat and turned it in his hands.

"What can I do for you Lewis?"

"I need to speak with Jenna Higgins." He turned the hat again and averted his eyes from Keesha. Lewis's walkie-talkie emitted some static and said, "Lewis, have a ten-five in downtown Social Circle at the Seven-Eleven. Mack and Jason will be there in five."

He pushed down the button. "I hear you Sherriff, I will be there soon."

"Now what could Jenna have done? She's no rabble-rowser I know that she has achieved her GED in less than three months. Real smart that one. We call her a keeper." Keesha pulled a nail file out of the drawer and softened the edges to the art she had applied to red nails. She had found some henna art online and redone it on her nails. She found everyone found her art interesting and liked to 'updo' some of the little things in life. It kept her mind busy. If she wasn't reading, she was creating art in as many spaces as she could find.

Jojo stood behind Keesha at the photocopier. Today she wore a dark blue tank dress with pearls and she had left her suit jacket at her desk due to the heat. She was photocopying another employee's recent Associate degree for the file. She had a frown and eyed the policeman with suspicion. She found other little things to do in the receptionist area, hoping Jenna would return soon so she could figure out what was going on.

"Oh no Ma'am. I'm not thinking poorly of her." He gave her a big smile back and both ladies acted troubled and immersed in thought. He thought maybe these ladies were more interested in Jenna's private lives then they should be. He didn't want to say much more.

But then Keesha picked up the phone. "Miss Jenna. You have a visitor. Hmmm hmmm. A cop here to in-vest-i-gate you. He looks very serious, but a little nervous too." Keesha emphasized investigate, pronouncing each syllable with a pause.

Jenna had been back in records doing some filing. She was troubled by this news and worried that it was about Josie.

She appeared back in the reception area, nervous and smiling before the policeman. She locked eyes with the man and shied immediately, averting eyes and feeling a pleasant stir in the pit of her stomach like hunger, but more spiritual. He had dark hair and light eyes, a clean, neat appearance and honest, straight-forward expression. Jenna had never seen his like before, though he seemed vaguely familiar. Though, she instantly again thought about Josie. He had come to take Josie to the Department of Human Services.

"Uh. Hi." He stammered. He turned his hat in his hands again.

Jenna was likewise floored and didn't know what to say or how to react. Double that with the fact that she was worried he had bad news and Jenna felt turned inside out. Things weren't working correctly in the quick-witted thought department, and her internal Manager was out to lunch. She didn't want more bad news and thought she might ingest the news like gunpowder for a firecracker and self-implode in front of the nice man.

"I know Lew from church." Keesha admitted then looked from one to the other, waiting for one of them to speak. Jojo couldn't find what she was looking for, because she wasn't really looking for anything. And Lewis the cop had turned pink-faced and was looking like a skewered pig ready for poking.

"I just wanted to check in on you and make sure you're ok. I mean with the horse and the x-boyf –, and the little girl –, your drunk mom and all. I don't know. I got a little worried about you." He was suddenly embarassed he had an audience and also that he told so many personal things about Jenna in such a public place. Maybe she didn't recognize him from the scene of Sven's crime either? "Sorry to bring that up in front of everyone. I saw you in my Spanish class and remembered you from that night with the horse. Oh jeez." He gulped. He was much better at keeping people's secrets to himself with the general public.

Jenna gulped and nodded. Jojo mumbled something unintelligible, and quickly vacated the reception area. She clearly did not want to get involved with Jenna's personal life.

Lewis turned his hat in his hands some more. He had divulged too much in front of Jenna's boss. Why didn't he just ask how she was? He felt silly.

A five minute pregnant pause of silence interrupted all conversation. Lewis's cheek blazed with embarrassment.

Keesha felt something needed to done, or said to help this situation. Clearly these two were too shy for their own good. "Hey Lew, Jenna…Ralph and I are going out to Peanuts Barbecue on Saturday. You and Jenna want to come along? We are bringing our daughter too. Jenna you kin bring Josie."

Lewis thought about this, scratching his head and readjusting his glasses. The static on his talkie blared again. "Lewis, you need a date … desperately … <chuckle> Ask the girl out and learn to turn your walkie-talkie off properly before doing personal things. You have work to do at the Seven-Eleven. Ten four."

Lewis unjammed the button from his talkie and cursed lightly under his breath. He blushed and nodded to both ladies. "That sounds good Keesha. You, um, available, Jen?"

"Sure." Was all Jenna could squeak out. She eeked out a smile and waved goodbye, feeling childish and simple, but giggling under her breath at the walkie talkie.

Once Lewis left, Keesha almost fell on the floor laughing. "Jenna, you are so shy and he is so shy and that was hil-air-ious! If I hadn't done something, you both would have said hello and gone about your own merry ways, wishing and hoping to see each other again. Lewis is one of the cutest bachelors in town. You are very lucky. I wouldn't let just any man go out with you. No, you are my friend now. I keep my friends safe and want the best for them."

Jenna was still feeling shy, but emerged as herself, more relaxed. "He was way too cute for me Keesha. I'm afraid he's too good looking and way too nice!" Jenna felt like she was sweating a little in response to Lewis's conversation.

Lewis re-emerged hearing their conversation, nervous. "Forgot my walkie-talkie." He was a brighter pink in the face and had obviously heard the conversation. He grabbed his walkie-talkie and then couldn't decide which way to leave from. Finally, he made a choice and almost ran out of the room.

Keesha laughed through her teeth and closed the window to the lobby. "He heard us." She whispered loudly to Jenna who pretended not to notice, but then they both giggled after trying to hold it all in. Jenna was better adjusted now.

Keesha hugged her and started a little ballroom dance with their hands up in the air. "Isn't love grand. Isn't it nice to feel cared for?" Keesha stole a side-glance at Jenna and in her best Cheshire grin, set about her work, planning for

Saturday night. Her nails chinked the keyboard keys as she googled, "best chocolates and gifts with barbecue." She would keep her professor in the loop.

Saturday night rolled around quicker than expected. Josie had brought home a craft project – a chicken made of corn and grain seeds glued to paper, which Jenna proudly put on the refridgerator. Jenna had also received a post-card from the Chief. He had hiked up through Ohio and was looking for old sacred sites of his ancestors, the Mingo Indian tribe of the Iroquois Confederacy. He was doing better, but still missed Ma. His card said that he hoped to be back in a week to help with the house – or horse – she couldn't read his writing, but assumed it to mean horse. Jenna was starting to avoid calling the Department of Human Services. She was fine with them taking their time since she was getting very attached to Josie. Josie hadn't brought up Sven or her momma in over eight months now. Jenna wasn't used to motherhood though and it came with it trials and tribulations.

One such event of discomfort reared it's ugly head when Josie realized that G and Butterball (now named because of how fat he had become) had a special connec-tion. The horses were fast friends and unfortunately G liked Butterball a little too much, but that was better than not at all. Jenna found herself covering Josie's eyes far too much and of course, one day, Josie asked the inevitable question.

"Jin, what is that thing between G's legs and why he like B's behind so much?"

"Oh, um, hon, that's what some boy horses like to do." Jenna's eyes widened and she sucked in some air, letting go and thinking about what to say further.

"It seems like a weird thing to do when you like someone. It doesn't look comfortable." Josie looked at them sideways. "And why does B pee?"

She asked Josie to go get the pants off the laundry line and called Keesha immediately. Red light! This seemed way too soon for such questions. She was not experienced in these matters.

"Already?! She's too young to be asking about that!" Keesha laughed, but there was concern in her voice.

"Well, we got these two horses, both boys and one pees, kinda teases G, and then, well you know G mounts the other ... Josie is curious. And these horses are so ... active."

"Um, Jin. Boy horses don't pee for the other horse." Keesha had grown up on a horse farm in Athens. Her family had owned a large estate.

"Damn!" Butterball was fat for a reason. Jenna immediately cringed at her use of an expletive. *Another vet bill*, was her immediate thought.

"Is Josie near you? Do you cuss like that near her?"

"No."

"Ok, good. See you at seven pm tonight, my friend. I called Lew and told him the time for you. I told him that he better respect you. He'll be picking you and Josie up too. Are you ok with that? – I know him, he's a good guy. We will definitely talk about the horses later. You'll call the vet tomorrow I hope?" It was a small town, and of all people, Jenna trusted a young and well-meaning policeman that she had relied on at the scene of Sven's crime.

Jenna nodded numbly.

"What about the horses?" Josie beamed up at Jenna. She carried the clothing. Jenna hoped the situation would change course.

"We will talk about it soon ok."

"Ok, soon."

The policeman. Oh, no, the policeman.What would she wear. Josie smiled and brought around her nicest flower dress.

"Jenna, kin you wear this?"

"Sure dear." It was perfect. She put Josie in a clean pair of pants she had found at Super-Mega-Mart's now successful competitor (since Super-Mega-Mart had not opened back up in months – the lot was a wasteland), and a nice pink tee. She braided josie's hair, and wiped a warm washcloth over her face. Josie put some lipstick on Jenna and accidentally smeared it on her cheek, giggling. Jenna grinned, fixing the mistake, and added powder to her face. She gave Josie a big hug and the two sat on the couch, nervous, anticipating the obvious.

"Jenna, I like you better than my momma."

"Oh, sweetie." Jenna started to cry, which confused Josie.

"I try to not be difficult." Josie pleaded with her. Jenna smiled through a wet face.

"Oh, sweetie, it's not *that*, I love you dear. You're not difficult. I'm just afraid your mama will want you back soon. I'm afraid I've gotten used to you and now you'll leave me." Jenna had had enough bad luck. It was such a comfort to actually have a friend and someone to take care of. She felt like Josie was a part of her life, a puzzle piece in a small neat puzzle that summed up her life's purpose. She hoped she could do better with Josie than her mama had done with her. She was still struggling with her mother's death. Her mother's trailer had been sold and Jenna had put the income into a savings account for expenses for Josie. Jenna still felt guilty though, hoping she had done what her mother wanted, still trying to impress her mother after her death. Her rage at her mother's death had quieted.

Josie no longer reminded her of Sven. For reasons she couldn't explain, it seemed that Josie belonged with her, that she was her responsibility. Though she had not birthed the child, she felt that the child was related to her somehow. Josie was now separate from Sven too. She had to be strong for Josie and care for Josie.

"Jin, kin you be my mamma now?"

"We'll see sweetie. I would like to be your mother, but I cannot promise anything." She hated that she couldn't just say yes. Josie made Jenna realize how much she wanted to be a mother, to be her mother.

Jenna was nervous about her date with Lewis since he was the first date she had had since Sven. She worried that she had bad luck with men but wondered if Lewis might be the one to break the curse. She was out of practice with dating and wasn't confident in herself about how to act. Though, she was feeling better about herself and had lost considerable weight. When she saw herself in the mirror she had noticed she was more confident. She also seemed to understand more of the words spoken around her at the community college. She felt smarter and felt she liked herself more.

The bird clock chirped seven pm and a sudden knock at the door disrupted their conversation. Jenna quickly cleaned up their faces and reapplied some powder to both of them. Lewis stood on the doorstep and she could see him through the mesh screen as she opened the door. He was wide-eyed and clearly ruffled, but more at ease than before. He looked different out of uniform, more human, and more approachable, even huggable. He wore a clean pair of dark blue jeans and a button up plain blue shirt.

He softened at the sight of Jenna and brightened at the sight of Josie. "Hi Jin. Josie!" Josie giggled and hid behind

Jenna's legs. Jenna noticed some powder on her shirt and wiped it off, beaming at Lewis.

He held a package of Belgian chocolates in his hand. "Keesha said you liked these?"

Jenna laughed and put them on the counter. Keesha was so funny. Just like her to have a man get Jenna chocolates. "Thank you so much. Truth be told, Keesha likes chocolates, but it's nice, her looking out for me."

"Oh, sorry Jenna. I thought flowers, but Keesha said that a good woman appreciates good chocolates." He gave a nervous grin.

"No, no, no, I love them, I do." She gave him a hug. He felt electric to her. She wanted to kiss him, hold him tighter, but it wasn't proper and it was too soon, so they distanced from each other, Josie deliberately sitting in the way in the middle of the couch. The blue and pink flowers on her dress matched Lewis's blue shirt and Josie's pink polo. His eyes scanned her face and though he was a little nervous, he clearly like to look at her. And she looked at him and smiled. He put his hands on knees and she wished his hands could be on her hands. She liked his touch. He smelled good too – nice and clean.

"Well, I guess we should go." Lewis walked with them to the door. His hand lingered on Jenna's back and she felt his breath on her hair. There was some sort of weird electric connection between the two of them. It had something to do with her soft skin and his soft skin intermingling in his wonderful touch.

At Peanut's, Keesha was a right riot. They sat at a picnic table indoors and the hum of the dust-laden air conditioner unit in a nearby window buzzed in on the conversation. The clapboard siding was steady, but the building was old and seemed to lean one way a little. The boards were old gray wood. It hadn't been painted in a while. And it's tenants had smoked one too many cigarettes and seemed over-worked, overtanned and a little tired. There were a few students there too. The place smelled of barbecue and sweet rolls, and a little smoke filled the room. Keesh told crazy stories about her Ralph, but Ralph and Lewis were not very chummy.

"Policemen make Ralph nervous, but he'll get over it. This is good for Ralph. No reason to have a problem with Lewis." Keesha said it outright in front of all of them. Ralph shifted in his seat but smiled as he took a napkin out of the dispenser next to the ketchup and salt and seasoned pepper. "He goes to our church, Ralph." She raised her voice emphasized 'church' it as if that was enough, and Ralph should get used to Lewis at that moment, right there. She had said it with finality. She was almost angry at him.

Keesha told them about the time Ralph had booked her a day at a special spa which had chocolate sauce on the spa menu. Little did innocent Ralph know, it was not a place of good repute. Keesha got mad at Ralph, thinking he'd been there, and she had run out of the spa, screaming, half-naked, with a dozen packets of chocolate sauce and a cancelled visa bill. "I can't say that was a good experience, but at least I almost made brownies. But … then we wouldn't have been able to eat them, cause who knows where that chocolate sauce had been." Her ample bosom giggled with her. Ralph grinned.

"How'd you two first meet?" Keesha just said it outright. She had no fear.

"Well, it wasn't under the best circumstances," Lewis admitted. "Sven had nearly killed the horse in Jenna's pasture, and I had to arrest him."

Jenna remembered Lewis's CHIPS glasses and his calming way with her on that day. She remembered his hand on her shoulder and the smell of fried okra.

He'd noticed Jenna that day too, but then thought of her more once he saw her in his Spanish class. She seemed like a nice girl who worked hard. Turns out he'd seen her at Super-Mega-Mart a couple times too, well before her Job at SCC. Lewis had noticed Jenna more than Jenna had realized. She felt so unattractive at Super-Mega-Mart. Funny how life turns around when you start feeling better about yourself, no matter how you are. "Then her Ma died. Oh gosh, there I go imparting more information."

"It's ok. We all know her Mom died. It's ok, baby. It's a small town." Keesha put a hand on his arm.

Lewis looked off uncomfortably.

"It hasn't hit me yet." Jenna admitted. "We started to get close, but I think it's best I not talk about it for a while."

Water welled up in Josie's eyes and she wiped her eyes and sniffled lightly. "She was a nice lady." Josie admitted. "And I miss the Chief." Zeena pulled Josie to another table to play tic tac toe on a small gamepiece made for such games. Josie was serious and slow, with her chin tilted down, but went along. She has holding back her emotions.

Jenna didn't like to talk about herself too much. But she felt boring and bland with this handsome man by her side and didn't know quite what to say. She also did not want to run him off by complaining.

Lewis leaned forward, his blue eyes on Jenna, and started a better tangent, "Have I told you about the time Tweena ended up in old Doc Barnhart's house, five miles away, in nothing but her shift, and he had to put a restraining order on her, over and over? She ended up in jail for it for a couple of days. She kept thinking he was her husband and told him they had unfinished 'business' in the corn patch. Wouldn't leave him alone. Bout near scared old Barnhart to pieces, but then they both single, having outlived their spouses by twenty years, and two months later they both found love in each other and Tweena is right happy." They all knew the story from a very outgoing Tweena, but laughed anyway. They knew he could only impart public information. There had also been a piece in the newspaper about Tweena. "Barnhart says if things don't work out, he'll just ressurect the restraining order." Doc Barnhart was the vet's father. He was in his nineties and still doing well, despite his age. Tweena had lived in Doc Barnhart's house when she was in her thirties and they thought maybe she was getting confused, since she had then later lived in the house her husband had built for the help, the house she kept leaving to visit old Doc Barnhart.

Chapter 6
G Love's Special Sauce

If you don't know what you're doing, how can you even know you made an error?

– Chief Proverb

"Which vet did a physical exam on this horse?" Dr. Barnhart (the younger) was yelling over the phone. "No, boy horses don't stand on their hind legs and pee for the other horse!" he stated with finality. "And that's NOT a harmonious relationship at all. The foal is likely too big for Buttercup and will kill Buttercup without intention to do so. We might need to do an early intervention. Did you not know that boy horses pee with a penis and girl horses pee by parting their legs? Didn't you notice that G Love and Buttercup pee differently?" He was angry but quickly changed this tone. According to the vet, girl horses and ponies also would pee as a form of flirtation. Josie did not hear this news, thank goodness. She was glad he had called her about this. She didn't think explaining horse body parts and horse sexuality to a young girl would be good idea at this time.

Jenna also knew nothing of horses, except that they required hay, grain, a pasture, and were expensive animals to own. She also knew that purchasing Buttercup had been a big mistake given her resources, but it had been an important bonding opportunity with her ma and with Josie. Yes, she should not have purchased Buttercup, but what was done was done and it had had some good effects overall.

The facts were as such: G Love gave new meaning to his name and needed to have his "special sauce" separated from the little B or he needed to be fixed (for everyone's safety), "and you really shouldn't own a stallion anyway – they're difficult to board, own and keep under control," the vet emphasized. Butterball was a she, not a he. Horse It All just wanted to sell them the damn horse. I mean her twenty years of knowledge should have imparted some sense of sexual differences between animals. In Horse-It-All's defense, Jenna remarked that maybe they could have noticed, but B was so low to the ground and so fluffy that nothing could be seen. She also had so much fat down there that it looked like something existed, it really did, but when touched, they matted down like the hairballs that they were and squished real easy, the vet pointed out with a smirk. So Buddy became Betty. And the vet came out to see what was going on. Sure enough Betty was very very pregnant, and they were happy that their attempts at dieting her had been unsuccessful. Apparently, the baby would be too big for Betty and they would have to do special surgery, eventually. Josie didn't mind that she couldn't ride her any longer. The vet told them, Betty might not make it. This baby could kill her. Betty was immediately shipped off by a student who had looked at the pony, then looked up at the angry beast, a little confused, then a little dismayed (on some days, G appeared to have red eyes), speeding off with the pony in a small trailer, off to the vet school, where her care would be less expensive than a traditional vet facility, but effective (hopefully). G Love galloped back and forth in front of the fence that faced the road. He was working up a sweat. He did not like to be without his Betty.

Jenna called Michelle at Meadowbrook and told her the bad news. This put Michelle on the defensive and Michelle said that her coggins stated that Buddy was a male. She was too busy to be checking all her horses – she didn't feel she had time to argue with the vet. But a coggins isn't supposed to be a physical exam, Jenna had told Michelle. Did you do any phsyical exams? Michelle had promptly squeeked a goodbye and hungup. Horse It All. Good thing they had rescued Butterball. Bad thing they had rescued her too. They all hoped it would work out. Especially Josie. Jenna also wondered about Michelle's comment when they had purchased Buddy. In a conversation when purchasing Buddy Michelle had noted the former owner had told her he was "good with stallions." She wondered if Michelle hadn't caught on to the fact that they might have meant Buddy was breedable.

G Love was a mess at the departure of Betty. He didn't eat, he pranced, he tried to break out of the fence. He really despised Jenna these days and she was getting tired of his shinanigans. Really, this horse needed to take a chill pill. Butterball would not be back for some time. The Vet School was deciding whether and when to have Betty have this baby that would be too big for her and Jenna worried about what the neighbor would think – more horses?!# Two was obviously the neighbor's limit, not three. She had a few months to try to sort things out with the neighbor. The vet was going to try to have Butterball keep the foal as long as possible and then extract it when necessary. He had also talked about castrating G Love. Jenna was afraid he'd hurt the vet though, and she was still pondering castration.

Jenna told all of this to Keesha the next day at work. Keesha was happy to have her facts confirmed.

"I mean it's possible a boy horse will act like a girl, but female horse intuition is much better than our own human instincts and I have not ever seen a boy horse pee to tease a stallion. Perhaps it's possible." She wore a dark brown sundress with beautiful black glass beads sewed along the edges.

Keesha changed the subject, cocking her head sideways. "Probably a silly question, but do you like Lewis?"

"Wow, Keesh, you don't skate around the issues, do you?"

"Umm, no." Keesha laughed and the chair shook a little adding to her beautiful momentum.

She'd seen him four times now and each time, he had allowed Josie along. "I like him a whole lot Keesha. I have to take it slow though. I have the horses, this little girl, and the man that my mom was dating is coming back. I don't know – I like him bettter and better on each date."

Keesha's brows furrowed. "Why is your mom's old man coming back? Is her your father?"

"No blood relative. He's a good guy, he's returning to help is all."

"Ok, but do tell me if Keesha needs to have a talk with him. You deserve to be safe, Jenna. But I know you're smart too." Keesha would refer to herself in third person when she talked tough.

"Thanks, I will. You're a good friend, Keesha. It's nice to have a good friend. Thanks for the compliment too."

A happy-go-lucky Lewis showed up from around the corner, donning the 80s glasses Jenna remembered from the fateful day. "Hi Jenna." He was more at ease now that they had gone out a couple of times. Jenna went through the small door to the lobby area and gave Lewis a big electric hug. He wavered over her forehead and she felt the warmth of his breath on her, he smelled like Lever2000 with a hint of mustard. He was not in uniform, but carried a pager and his walkie-talkie, just in case. He had made sure the button was not stuck down each time he saw Jenna.

"You have mustard on your shirt." Jenna got a napkin and tried to get some of it off.

"Oops. I am such a dunce. I grabbed a quick hotdog from the cafeteria. Musta dribbled some mustard on me when I was eating it."

He started to help with the napkin and touched Jenna's hand. Goosebumps raised on her arm. "No worries, happens to all of us." Jenna said in a deep breath.

"I thought I'd stop by after class. Do you want to study and order pizza tonight? We have that big test on Thursday."

Jenna didn't know if she could afford a babysitter and she didn't know if he minded Josie being around. She thought and didn't say anything for a moment. "Can we study at my trailer?"

"I was thinking you could bring Josie to my condominium and all three of us could study there. We have a nice little play area with a swingset and kiddie pool. Some of the neighborhood kids play there."

Jenna didn't like this at all, at the same time, she liked it too well. It was a paradox. She'd like him even more after seeing his place. He was so clean cut and well put together. She imagined his place to be even nicer than him and she imagined herself falling for him, and then like Sven, he'd lose interest and leave her with more bills and a heartache the size of a few local towns. And she and her trailer were so messy, and her trailer was so cheap and falling apart.

She realized Keesha was frowning at her. Best she start to let go of the past.

"Ok, Lewis." *But, I'm scared,* she'd wanted to say.

"Pick you both up here at work tonight? I'll bring you home at a decent time too. I don't aim to keep you out late. I know you have a few things to do with work, school, horses … etc … " His eyes twinkled when he said late, and Jenna knew he'd wanted to keep her out late with him and she knew that she wanted that too. *Oh lord, I'm falling, I'm falling I tell ya and I'm afraid I won't get up* she thought.

"You'd have to pick us up at my trailer, Lewis. We have to feed G." An image of G dancing and pacing at the fence for breakfast and the possible return of the Butterball surfaced in her mind. An image of Lewis, shirtless, in her mind too. Erase image of Lewis, and replace with image of feeding the sweating stallion.

"Oh, yep, that makes perfect sense. That way you have your car at home too, not left here at work. I wasn't thinking." He was so nice. But wait, was he thinking they would stay over for the night? That wouldn't be right for Josie.

He recognized the cogs turning in her head. "No, no, Jenna, I didn't mean for you both to spend the night or nothing, that wouldn't be right. I mean, well, it'd be too soon. Or … I think … ummm … "

Jenna didn't laugh, but she wanted to at first. Then she realized he was scared too. Nice guy like him had probably dealt with mean girls.

"See you at 6pm at my trailer to pick me and Josie up." Lewis vacated quickly, looked a little perplexed.

Bad news awaited her at home.

Josie ran to the trailer first, after noticing Chief's cane leaning against the door.

Josie jumped up and down. "Chief is back! Chief is back!"

"But I took a nasty fall from G-Grumps." Chief said from the couch, not moving much, but breathing just fine.

Jenna stated "We missed you Chief." Much had changed since they had last seen the Chief. "I have a new job now." And a new man and new friends, she thought, not wanting to jinx her new relationships.

Jenna and Josie both hugged him. He was stoic and quiet but they could see a tear well up in both his eyes. The wrinkles on his face appeared emotional to them, though nothing appeared to move. His face was full of experience and knowing. He uncharacteristically hugged them tight. He was warm and smelled like pipe tobacco and cinnamon.

"How have you been Grandpa Chief?" Josie looked up at him with big eyes. A tear rolled down her cheek and she sniffled. She hugged his leg as if she wouldn't let him to leave again.

"Oh wandering in the wilds my young one." The Chief put a hand to her shoulder, warm and comforting.

Jenna felt a sense of calm and responsibility with this man as if he would take care of everything. He was a very trustworthy soul, dependable to her and her mother before her.

Jenna inhaled though, worried about his recent fall. *No hospital visits please*, Jenna thought to herself.

He had obviously found the hidden key and let himself in, but Jenna knew that the Chief could always be trusted. Ma had never had good taste in men until Chief and she just knew he was good. He was always fixing things, animals and trailer alike. "Grumps is a stubborn one, but I'm ok." The Chief barely lifted his head, and an empty soup bowl was on the coffee table next to him. "Didn't break nothing, just sore. He's real mad about his pasture-mate."

G had bucked the Chief off in the canter. He was doing the walk and trot fine, but got excited in the canter, or she thought maybe his leg still hurt, but the Chief confirmed it – G was just feeling good and testing the Chief. Jenna found that she yearned to ride a horse and couldn't figure out where it came from. Luckily, it was now mixed in with some common sense too. This thing had hurt the Chief.

"That horse was like an acrobat. I swear his feet went over his head." Chief exclaimed.

The Chief mumbled something about castrating the horse (Jenna could swear she saw the horse lift his head from the field at this comment) and Chief laughed – though Chief seemed to hurt when he laughed.

The men in her life seemed much more emotionally healthier these days. Lewis was an Adonis to her sure. But it seemed her heart was too fragile for her heart to hurt or leave her now very functional family environment. It's funny how things always balance themselves out. You find someone good and there are always other good forces competing with each other, whether deliberate or not.

Lewis arrived at the door, this time with flowers. "Hi Jenna." He nodded at Josie, and then his stare settled on the Chief. He was used to wondering about people's motives. He wasn't sure where this Native American man had come from. Jen could see the worry on his face. His smile faded.

Jenna opened the door, the smell of chicken soup danced out of the door.

Who's this?" He went to tip his hat and realized that he was out of uniform, he was so used to his hat.

"I'm Chief." Josie bounced on the Indian's knee and laughed. He couldn't be all bad if Josie liked him.

"You new to these parts?"

"Oh no. In a way, I consider myself Josie's grandfather."

Lewis sighed inwardly. "Oh, a blood relative." It made sense.

"No, no…I was Vera's boyfriend, you know Jenna's ma – her boyfriend." He seemed used to explaining himself calmly to people. A calm way about him.

"Jenna, you ok with this guy just hanging out?" Lewis didn't know what else to say to Chief. The man seemed to like the quiet better than talking. Josie ran into her room and arrived at the door with a few books. Jenna carried her notebook and her purse. Jenna seemed to glow, her hair pulled back into a pony tail.

"He's fixed up my place, Lew, and he took care of Ma, stood by her during the hard times. He means no harm, and he's helping with that crazy horse in the pasture. Josie trusts him too."

Chief had no interest in the matter and did not look at them as he rested on the couch. "I'll watch Josie." The Chief stated it then looked to Jenna. "You sure you ok driving off with this guy?"

"I wanna go with Jenna!" Josie frowned and stamped her foot.

"Little one, don't you want to hear how Buttercup is doing? Do you want to help me make peace with Grumps?" The Chief looked downtrodden, a little depressed.

Clearly Josie wanted to know about Buttercup.

"Don't have have Josie interact with G." Jenna stammered, worried about Josie interacting with the stallion, "but I bet she'd like to hear about Buttercup." She turned Josie's face up and traced a smile on her face. Jenna felt funny leaving Josie behind, but it would mean that Josie would go to bed on time, and that Jenna would have a night off. She loved Josie dearly, but lately felt like a constant mother, always responsible, always worrying about dear Josie. It would be nice to have her in safe hands for the evening, while she did something for herself – just this one thing for now. She knew the Chief didn't trust Josie with with Lewis more than Lewis didn't trust them with the Chief. And besides, Lewis smelled so good to her. He made her feel good too. Granted, she would not start ignoring Josie for this beautiful man, but she did want to spend some quality time with him for one evening. She was a little nervous being alone with Lewis for the first time, but also had been thinking about when it would happen – her excitement overcame any nervousness she felt and she told herself "I deserve this." She deserved a little peace in her tumultuous life.

They hopped in Lewis's black Honda Accord and sped to his condominium. His car was clean and smelled new. The band 'Coldplay' blared a sinewy whine from the stereo and Jenna suddenly felt more contemporary. Did she look like a farmer trailer park girl? She hated to worry about where she came from, but feared that Lewis was a whole new world. She was afraid he would ask her about Josie. About whether the Department of Human Services had been in contact with her. About what her intentions with Josie were –to adopt or not? Afterall, not a lot of men want a girl- friend and a child at the same time. So far he had seemed fine with Josie, but she wondered if the two of them became serious if having a child to care for would be an issue with him. He drove fast and Jenna realized that she was holding onto the armrest with her nails dug into the vinyl. Ooops. They ran a couple of yellow turned red lights. Her knuckles were white with anxiety. Weren't cops supposed to be the best drivers? He clearly drove with a great deal of speed but at least some precision. Cops critique everyone else's driv- ing…She turned the music down a little and grinned at Lewis. He scanned her face and seemed to settle his gaze on her lips. *Behave yourself Jenna, behave,* she thought. Was he paying attention to the road? Was he showing off for her? He seemed to have a lot of energy, and she felt it directed at her. What was the rule for intimacy? Four dates? She felt more comfortable with four months after the Sven ordeal. And she remembered that horrible skanky woman without teeth or underwear. She shuddered. What kind of woman had Lewis dated before her? Why did she ever go out with Sven in the first place?

At the condominium, Jenna found herself amazed at the size of his home. There wasn't a whole lot of furniture, but it looked comfortable, spacious, and modern. It was a bachelor pad, complete with futon and stereo system. Everything was beige. Even the countertops were beige. There was no dust, and the television screen appeared free of dust. The carpet looked new and was a light tan (almost beige). This place was the visual equivalent of Switzerland: neutral. She looked at all his books and noticed a few series: lots of battle and war books. Sun Tzu's "Art of War," Ken Follett's books sat on the clean shelves. She wondered if he had the book by Ken Follett that she had read last year. It was called, "Lie Down with Lions," and was possibly the best book she had ever read. She still had it above the bed in the trailer.

"You like Ken Follett?" Jen touched the spines of the books. She was starting to appreciate books more and more. Afterall, her studybooks for the GED had helped her to pass the exam.

"Oh yeah. He's great. I loved 'Pillars of the Earth.' You can take it if you want to read it?" He pulled Pillars of the Earth out and handed it to her. She put it next to her purse on the old wooden coffee table in front of the beige couch. It was quite the heavy tome, a serious work of fiction. The table was nicked up a little, but looked antique. Her eyes traced the ornate knots in the side of the woodwork.

Lewis noticed her looking at it. "It's from my Aunt in Iceland. Our family has Icelandic origin. The pewter set in the kitchen is from Iceland too."

"Interesting." *I'm 100% country mutt*, thought Jenna.

Lewis put a tablecloth down, and he got them some ice water. They pulled out their Spanish books and set up everything on coffee table. Here in Georgia, ice was always in your drink, no matter what you had. The days of air conditioner units had cooled down places nicely, but you still always had ice in your drink to cool you down. And it was nice to see the glass sweat, it made the water seem all the more appealing.

"Alright, so Friday's exam is about masculine and feminine nouns." He pointed to himself. "This is easy, but el chico," he pointed her, touching her knee, "and la chica."

"We're living in the land of la libertad." Jenna laughed and held up her paper so he couldn't cheat.

"liberty – feminine noun. Super easy. What about el libro?"

"masculine of course and is it book?"

Lewis nodded and scooted closer. Jenna smelled fabric softener and some sort of light musky cologne. She gulped. Their eyes locked and she noticed he looked a little serious, intent. He seemed to see through her.

Within moments, his hand was on her neck and he was brushing his lips on her own. He smelled clean and she felt high. She brushed back, parting his lips with her own, running her tongue along his top lip. Then she pulled back a little, but he looked so pained, so determined. He held her tight against himself and shuddered as they kissed, deeper and deeper. His hands were under her shirt and on her back. Goosebumps like little mountains dotted her skin and she felt as some sort of static electricity charge within her.

"I'm scared, Lewis." Her eyes watered.

"I'll go as slow or as fast as you want me too." His body trembled with contained angst for her. She felt him pushing against her. "Your skin is so soft." He said, grinning. Then he charged her again. She was like the red flag and he the bull. Except there were no Spanish streets to run through, she clearly wanted this bull, and wanted him now. At the same time, she wanted his respect and his companionship and she didn't want to make a mistake, by letting him close in too fast. He took her shirt off and pulled her down onto the couch, flinging all of the schoolbooks away like crumbs on a picnic cloth. The coffeetable upended sideways and fell away with his swift push too. His lips were on her chest and her shoulders and he was towering over her and owning her, and she was giving in with all of her abilities, lost in the drunken swirl of him, of his power and love and intensity. He was becoming a determined bull, mad in his like of her, mad in his need for her. Jenna trembled and felt her body going soft, her body warming, as he started to undo her pants. The unbuttoning seemed to take forever.

"Is this too soon?" She bit her lip and put her hand down over her pants.

"If it's too soon for you, we can wait. I want you to feel right about me." Lewis held her head in his hands as he trembled. His hand was warm, her body felt heated, she wanted to give herself to him, but knew that she best wait a little while longer. He kissed her long and slow and proceeded to kiss her shoulders, her neck. He held her too him.

For once in her life, Jenna felt alive. She felt human. And she felt important. Lewis made her feel like a real person, and he respected her.

"Yes, Lewis. I really really like you. And that's why we need to wait. I want to make sure we're right for each other before I sleep with you. Is that ok?" Jenna wanted him, wanted him to take her, but she wanted to know this wasn't just lust first, that he was not Sven, that she could trust him.

"You're amazing, Jenna." They kissed for another few hours, ate some dessert and watched Discovery Channel reruns. They didn't get much studying in after all.

CHAPTER 7
ADRENALINE AND ANGER

Best to second guess all guesses and stick with the facts.
                                                    —Chief Proverb

She had been thinking of Lewis all day at work. Remembering, with a shudder, the night before. She felt at times guilty and winced inwardly at her inability to get intimate, and at times joyous at their closeness that evening. Parts of that evening played over and over, she ached with the thoughts of him. Despite her decision not to leave Lewis, she still worried about the relationship, that may have moved too fast for her liking.

A letter from the Department of Human Services (DHS) seemed to glow on the table like a Holy Grail of information. Jenna stared at it. Josie wondered what was so important about this letter. The Chief pretended as if it didn't exist. It seemed to float above the table and beckon to her in its simplicity, in its purpose, in its possibility of bad omens. She had studied it so much, she knew the font typeface and the logo for DHS.

"I'm not sure I can open it."

Josie was curious now about the letter too. "Maybe there's a bonus in it or something? Could it be about Buttercup?

What is it?" Josie's eyes were wide and she tried to read it. "D-E-P-A-R-T-M, Department....of..."

"Department of Human Services. It's about you dear. I'm afraid to open it. It could be bad news."

"Oh." Josie looked down at Chief and then went and curled up in his lap. He moved her to his good leg and brushed back her hair. Josie stared at the letter to now. It seemed to levitate on the table. Of course it didn't levitate, but with all the energy directed at it, it might as well have.

Jenna gingerly started to open it. She sighed and put it back on the table. She was afraid of this letter.

The phone rang. Josie was cuddled up on the Chief's lap staring at the letter as well.

"Uh, hi." Jenna answered, thinking it was Keesha, wondering how the date went. It was a bit late for Keesha to call.

Unfortunately for Jenna, it was far worse than a friend's call. "Why didn't you bring Josie around while I was in jail? What the fuck is your problem Jenna? You tarded or something?"

Jenna started to sweat. She thought she was rid of Sven. She thought he would be in jail for a long time. Was he calling her from jail?

"I do miss you Jenna, but only a tiny bit." She heard a bottle chink in the background. A woman talking to an animal. She wondered if it was Josie's mom. "Well, what the fuck you got to say for yourself?"

Jenna's eyes welled up but she toughened herself and dried her tears with sheer will. "How's jail?"

Sven laughed over the phone. A little static mixed in. "Ha ha Jenna. You don't stay in jail for punching a stupid animal. It's not like I was intending to do anything wrong. It's not like I ever done anything wrong." Jenna blinked in incredulation. She clearly remembered his threatening words at the Super-Mega-Mart. Heck yeah he had intended to do something. He had also already done so much wrong. Her new self knew he was entirely wrong. Her old self would have wavered.

"Ha ha yourself or you will be sorry. You stay away from us or I'll have you arrested again. I have a restraining order against you. You aren't allowed near any of us."

The Chief gently lifted Josie up and set her on the couch next to him. He removed Jenna's tight white knuckles gently from the phone and thought a moment with the phone facing down. The Chief was tired and beaten and this was not the altercation he had envisioned, thought Jenna.

"Jin, you bitch!!!!!!" They could both hear his deep alto from the phone.

He lifted the phone. "You will leave us alone." The Chief stated it as a directive rather than a statement.

"Who the fuck is this? Jenna got a new boyfriend? What the fuck you think you doing? I'm gonna fuck you up. You sound old. You bag of shit. I'm gonna git you and you gonna wish you never knew Jin. Put Jin on the phone. I got to talk some sense into her tarded skull."

The Chief pointed to Jenna and Josie to leave the room and they heard his muffled talk from the bedroom. "Mister. I saw what you did to horse. If your anger takes you over and you come over here again, then you will wish you hadn't."

"Who the fuck are you?"

"Don't mess with my family. Like Jenna told you: STAY AWAY. Jenna's stronger. We will deal with you." Jenna had never before heard the Chief raise his voice like this, nor had he spoken to her strength like this.

Sven laughed sarcastically and banged the phone against something. "You're tarded too you old fuck. You can have Jin. I just want what's mine. I'm coming over right now."

Jenna did not like all of the cussing coming out of Sven's mouth and she hoped that Josie had not heard the yelling cusswords over the phone. She was also angry at Sven's stupidity. Sven had just assumed the Chief was her new boyfriend.

Josie looked up at Jenna, concerned. "Sven has a bad attitude. Don't make me go back to him." Josie shook her head back and forth.

"We are taking good care of Josie." The Chief said it in the phone and then hung up, placing it back into the receiver.

"Jenna, you're gonna need to take Josie and get out of here, soon. I'll take care of the rest." He leaned on his cane and opened the screen door.

Jenna and Josie got into Jenna's Chevy. Chief closed their doors and patted the trunk. Jenna turned the key in the ignition, but her smelly heap of metal would not buck into life. Grumps snorted and did a little dance near their side of the fence. "Oh no. Not now." Jenna kept trying to get the car to start, but it just wouldn't. She panicked and started to vertigo slightly. "Oh no, not now." She was really late on her oil changes. She remembered one more bottle of oil she had in the trunk. The Chief opened the hood and Jenna opened the trunk, retrieving the oil. They poured the oil into the oil repository. With a dull thud, they closed the hood and Jenna tried once again to get her old Chevy to come alive. She had dark black oil smudges on her fingers, but she didn't care. She needed to get Josie out of here. It wouldn't work, wouldn't turn on. Maybe she should call Louis or Keesha, or just call the police. They might be fine, but Sven had a habit of getting angry and taking care of 'things' that he thought needed taking care of. He'd said he'd be right over and this was a small town.

Jenna's panic wasn't helping the situation. Chief told her to take some deep breaths and try and settle herself down. She felt stronger than she had before when she had dealt with Sven. Did the neighbor have a car she could borrow? No, the neighbor was not at home. Is there someone else she could call? Maybe that nice man that she had studied with? Her wits started to return to her.

She didn't want to bother Lewis or the police as they would inevitably involve him. Afterall, she'd just seen him, and this was the type of crisis he'd probably handle well, but she didn't want to be overbearing and all-consuming. Seeing him during this crisis would not help their relationship. It would be too soon and she didn't want Sven to hurt him or for him to do something to Sven that he'd regret. She called Keesha.

"Oh-yes,-hello-Keesha" became a single word as she gasped. "Sven might be coming to hurt us or something – you're so smart, do you have advice?" She squeaked it out as she heard the rumble of a motorcycle outside.

"What's going on –" Keesha was cut short by Jenna.

"Oh no…He's here." The phone dropped and hit a chair. Josie started to cry and ran to Jenna. Jenna held her close and stroked her hair. "It's ok baby, we will be strong." Chief put his cane next to the couch and went out the door.

"I think I know where G gets his personality from." Chief uttered it as he left as if he could also calm Sven's inner beast.

Jenna worried that perhaps Sven had the horsepower of more than one when he became angry. She spied Sven and Chief from the window. Josie was cutting off the circulation to her right arm and hand, but Jenna didn't know how to calm her. She herself had started to feel a pulse in her ears, like a great flood was gonna come and kill them all. Her emotions were starting to break through the dam as well. An image of her Ma in the emergency room popped up, red nails, red blood, too many sick people, and all of the horror of losing someone she cared for flooded to her as well. She held onto Josie tight too. "Dear Lord, keep this little girl safe." It was her mantra, she prayed it over and over. Good lord, what about Chief. She prayed for Chief too, who was obviously trying to talk Sven down. Josie's tears fell on her wrist. Josie whimpered like a little puppy, hurt and scared. Helplessness washed over Jenna.

But something started to bubble up in Jenna, some part of her that said, "NO, not this time." A wave of rage rumbled over her skin and she felt a jumpstart of the ignition within her belly. No, I don't think I'll let him take her, she thought. She thought of his motorcycle and of his smelly, sweaty face that needed a shave. Of the yellowed teeth and the eyes lost in layers of fatty adipose tissue and pimples. She thought of Josie having to spend time with this anathema, this pathetic man and she started to fume. It felt like smoke was building up, like a great volcano was bubbling. "Who the hell was he to take such advantage of her." She mumbled out loud. Josie was startled but still scared and whimpering. Josie seemed to sense her strength.

Outside, she saw Sven turn his head towards the mumbling. "Baby, go in the bedroom and lock the door. Don't open it until I tell you, ok sweetie?"

"ye-ah. Bu – t I'm sc–a–red." Josie stuttered it out into a longer sentence. Jenna lifted her, scooted her in the bedroom and told her again. "Lock the door sweetie, quickly. I will keep you safe. Don't worry honey."

The lock clicked.

"Try to be quiet. I'll take care of this."

"o–k." whimper.

What the hell was Jenna doing? Was she gonna let this man ruin her life? She'd started to get somewhere in life without him, with him behind bars and she wasn't going to let him drag her back down. She punched a wall and then realized it hurt, massaging her hand.

She stormed outside and stood next to the Chief.

"What the hell do you want, Sven?" Her bellow could probably be heard by the neighbor, had he been home.

"I came her to git what's mine." Jenna hoped he meant the horse.

"I'm sure as hell that the horse is yours."

"That's a fucker, that horse. I hate that horse. Josie's ma gave me that horse to kill me and I want it dead, I do." G let out a whinny and paced at the fence, kicking and pawing at the air. He sensed their nervous energy, and for once the horse and Jenna were on the same wavelength.

Oh dear goodness. Since when does someone buy a horse with the intention for it to hurt someone? That was just silly. Despite this crazy horse's mentality, Jenna knew from what the vet had said, that this was a stallion and stallions are mostly all like this: wild, crazy and they can be killers if put in the wrong situation. "So you gave it to me to kill me? That's just ridiculous." Jenna spat at him and stomped her feet. "I've had enough of you, Sven. I did nothing but help you and git you everything you wanted and here I watched this little girl. This little sweet thing that has done nothing wrong. And that damn horse. You think I want all this responsibility when I barely get to spend time with you, when I was treated like crap. Like you could walk all over me. No I realize you don't really deserve all this emotion out of me, but I'm pissed off as hell, and I am not taking it anymore!!!" Jenna put out her fists and put them in front of her.

"Jin, you look hot when you're mad. You lost weight?"

"Oh, hell no you are not getting into my pants, mother-fucker. You better get the hell off my property. I already called the police. I'm tired of you and I want you to leave us alone. The little girl has a good life here." Normally she would not cuss this much, but she had to fight fire with fire.

Sven started to redden. "That little girl's mine and I'm taking her now."

Jenna started to sputter and sweat and her hair stood on end. "Hell NO."

"Get her the fuck out here or I'm going to have to force you." He grinned with evil menace as he was not in the best of moods.

Jenna pushed him backwards and the Chief pulled her back.

"Look you fuckers. I worked things out with the Department of Human Services. They should have let you know I'd be calling. It's part of my parole." Sven seemed to deflate a little. "It's all well and legal and ain't no one keeping my daughter from me."

Jenna let go of some of the fury and anger that she had imbibed, and thought a moment about the letter on the table. The letter from the Department of Human Services. Had she read that letter, this whole event might have gone a lot smoother. She felt defeated, like a weight had been dropped on her head with the realization that her worst fears had come true. She felt hopeless and deeply concerned about Josie.

"No they wouldn't do that." Jenna deflated and felt smaller. "Besides I have restraining order on you."

Sven looked larger than he had previously. " 'Fraid so Jin. She's mine and nothin' you can do 'bout it. I ain't afraid of no restraining order."

"You don't love her though and you're not responsible enough to care for her." Jenna realized she was unable to worsen her vocabulary.

"You think you're smarter than me now?" Sven seemed to bristle and darken.

"I can contact the authorities and petition them. You can leave her here. She's in a good place and well cared for."

" 'Fraid not Jin."

"She's a daughter to me." Jenna pleaded with him.

"Yeah right. You got no motherly instinct, that's for sho Jin. You're a right riot today. Think you're smarter and better than me, using all your fancy new words on me. You think you know better. You don't. You still ain't nothing to me or nobody else."

"You don't know me at all then Sven. I don't know why I ever liked you. You're the riot, and I do know better and I am smarter than you." Jenna puffed up. "Oh Gawd. You ain't no better, really." He picked something out of his teeth. His stubble threatened to shoot off his face. Quarter size bags under his eyes showed that he was tired and angry. "Besides Josie has got some explaining to do to me too."

What problem could he have with a child. She grasped at anything to keep Josie away from him. She wasn't giving her to him. "You're not leaving here with her, unless you have a second helmet for her to get on the bike with you." She couldn't believe she was even going to let Josie on the bike. "And what do I do with that darn horse."

"Sell it for horse meat. I don't have no second helmet and I'm taking her."

Sven bust open the screen door and stormed through the house, heavy steps making the house groan and ripple. "Where the fuck is she?"

"Where the fuck is the helmet, or do you not care if she's safe?" Jenna realized she should check the letter to make sure Sven could take her. She opened it quickly and unfurled the paper from it's neatly folded self, it was typed and had a government seal at the top.

"We are sorry to inform you that Josie Stevenson must be returned to her father, Sven Stevenson, or else this will become a legal matter. Due to the restraining order in effect, DHS can take the child and transport her to ... " And then lots of legalese on timing, etc ... "Oh darn."

Sven turned the doorknob to the bedroom. The door didn't budge. Josie would need to go with Sven. "Open up."

"I don't wanna." A sniffle.

Jenna was hoping Sven wouldn't figure out Josie was in there.

"Open this fucking door you little twat! I'm gonna teach you who's daddy if you kin't learn it now." Oh lord, what a horrible vocabulary, what horrible thoughts he had.

"Sven. Do not use that language with her! She's a little girl. You have to be gentle with little girls."

"What? She needs a whipping." He spat at Jenna, but she wasn't afraid.

"Get the hell out of here Sven. You are not a daddy. You just aren't and you didn't even come prepared." She felt a little clostraphobic.

"I don't like to hit women, Jin. But you makin me real angry-like and I need this situation to be easier in about a minute." He lifted his finger and his lips were set in an angry line. He was impatient, but Jenna had made up her mind. Jenna punched him in the groin and quickly felt her knuckles to make sure that she was ok. They went numb for a little while, and then it smarted like someone had taken sandpaper and scoured her hands with it.

Sven's fury was about to overtake him so she stuck her fingers in his eyes and lifted her knees to catch him in the chin. Then, Chief dropped an old thick glass vase on his head. With a clunk it thudded on Sven's head. Sven growled and crumpled to the floor, like a bear, a big sweaty, smelly reddish white bear.

The Chief smiled. "Now he is sorry he messed with my family." The Chief appraised Jenna. "I didn't have to do much, you've become stronger and smarter Jenna." The Chief gave a strong hand to her arm and leaned on her. He was getting older and clearly not strong enough to deal with Sven, but she was strong enough to deal with him and had somehow dealt with him.

Jenna breathed out and instantly the pain of her confrontation became clear. Her knees felt pained, heavy, and they buckled. She was like a plastic blow-up raft suddenly devoid of all air. The eye defense had been a good idea though, as it had hurt her the least. Now what the heck were they going to do with this big gross man on their floor? They needed to think fast, otherwise, he'd wake up. She had been too embarrassed to call the police or Lewis, but she knew she needed to anyway. She finally realized she had to what was best for Josie and dialed the police. She also thought Sven needed more help. Breaking and entering was likely not legal. Also he was drunk when trying to pick up Josie, which would likely not be allowed by the Department of Human Services. She was suspicious of what benefits the Department offered to Josie, were they even interested in her living in a loving home? How had they thought she would be in a good situation with Sven?

"Yes, ma'am can you explain clearly what happened? Do you also need medical personnel?" She discussed the events with the police. "Oh yes ma'am, a lady named Keesha called us about this. We already have personnel on the way."

Hopefully, they hadn't killed him. She checked for a pulse on Sven as requested by the woman on the phone. He did have a pulse. He also appeared to be breathing. Sven also smelled like he'd had a lot of beer, so she guessed that the beer was clouding his judgement too and maybe he'd take a nice little nap. Another reason she did not let Josie on his motorcycle. Driving drunk and no helmet for the child. No way was she going with him.

There was something else she wanted to do. This whole event had lit a fire somewhere in her soul and she was determined to heal. Jenna opened the screen door and went to the pasture. The beast eyed her with an air of suspicion. She eyed the beast with an air of suspicion. He started to pace and rear and he showed her the whites of his eyes and fury in his soul. Jenna eyed him and stomped her foot, showing him her backside as she proceeded to undo the fence.

For a long moment the eye of G Love connected with Jenna's eyes. Instead of hatred, she saw passion and love in the horse's eyes. His soul was scarred because this beautiful animal had been abused and hated. Now this animal had changed, had known love. This horse was like a bruise that had now healed. She felt a strong connection to the animal. She felt the vibration of his strong eye as he continued to stare into her soul, his soul mingling with her heart. She shivered and she suddenly felt warm. Jenna stood up tall and leaned towards the horse. She lifted her chin and felt as if she herself might rear up. The skin on his back rippled in the moonlight. His beautiful scraggly mane rustled in the breeze as mighty magnificent eyed her with great horse angst. He was pregnant with anticipation. The beast knew some mighty moment had arrived.

He ran to the corners of the pasture. But he returned to a dead stop to stare her in the eye. He no longer needed to challenge her, challenge this castle, this yard. This was hers, he was hers. That little girl, she was now hers too. The trembling sweaty neighing braying beast kneeled down to her in a show of deference. The small light in his eye twinkled for freedom. He jumped on his hindquarters and neighed a horsely bellow into the wind. Where was his Buttercup? Didn't G Love deserve a relationship too?

Jenn understood him perfectly in that moment. The beast did a rear kick and took off like a demon out of hell, kicking up dust and rocks, nearly hitting the fence with his hooves but sailing freely over the fence. He put his head up high in the air, let out a bellow to tell her how he felt about the whole thing and ran, and ran, happy, free and like a majestic black force, hair whipping in the breezes, getting smaller and smaller as she saw him run over pastures. She had grown fond of the beast. And she would raise the girl, or find the girl's mother. She would help Josie, and Josie certainly did not deserve Sven.

Chief smiled from the doorway. "It was time Akwenoi achieved his freedom. I'm sure someone else will have better resources – he'll not get far and we don't have major roads out here, so he's relatively safe." Jenna would call the Humane Society shortly to report the horse. She didn't think he was dangerous anymore. The Chief had calmed him considerably. She was hoping he would find his Buttercup. Maybe there was a mare somewhere for G. She loved G and wanted the best for him. She knew she would look for him in every field she saw. Her wild G. Josie's wild G. The Chief may not look for him though, he seemed like an unruly teenager to the Chief.

Jenna breathed, relieved. What a beautiful day it was. A beautiful day to be happy. The moon shown down brightly on the scene and Jenna noticed the stars too. A large meteor sailed overhead and Jenna wondered if that was ma, telling her, "good job, baby."

Now, what to do with Sven. There had to be a solution to this problem. Jenna went to the bedroom. "Josie open up. Sven's passed out." Josie clicked the lock and opened up the door.

"I didn't want to go with Sven." Josie stepped over Sven.

"We didn't want you to go with Sven either." Jenna looked at the Chief, who was back on the couch, resting. He was clearly very tired. Jenna wanted to keep an eye on Sven while she waited for the police.

"I'm sorry you had to hear that honey. Hitting other people is not ok."

"Momma you saved me from him. He was never nice to me." Josie leaned on Jenna.

"He didn't have good intentions." In the future she should also immediately call the police and find a neighbor. Handling these situations herself was getting exhausting but she was becoming stronger too.

"Nothing good about my daddy." Josie looked sad.

"You are so much kinder than him, luckily you inherited all the best qualities." Jenna smiled.

"Thank you for sticking up for me, for caring about me." Josie smiled up to Jenna.

"Wow, Jenna. You um- weren't going to let him get any-where near Josie." Keesha and her husband stood over Sven in the hallway.

"No." Jenna stated it as fact.

They looked at each other, the letter from the Department of Human Services dangling from Keesha's hand. Keesha and Ralph had rushed over after Jenna's phone call. They were stopped at a police checkpoint to check I.D.'s and insurance and traffic had been a little backed up. Luckily, they had run into Lewis at the checkpoint and told him what was going on. Lewis stood behind the two of them, protective and angry, but with his feelings under control, wondering what could be done as well. Logic said that the little girl should not go to this crazed drunken motorcycle driver. He wondered how he hadn't heard about this. Jenna told him that Keesha had called the police a while back. It turned out that there was another emergency at the Super-Mega-Mart. A body had been found in the building while demolition crews were there to haul away parts of the building. A clipboard had been found on the man. In addition, there was a major accident on a local road.

He made some phone calls to try to help with Josie.

"Hi Lew. Legally, he is her father. It appears he has done some things that are neither appropriate nor legal, but he has rights too as her father."

Lewis sighed. He could research this guy, or have some words with him, but knew based on what he already knew about him, that much of his words and research would be useless. He called the Department of Human Services.

"Department of Human Services, Administration, How can I help you?"

"We have Sven Stevenson here and he stormed a house against a restraining order to get Josie Stevenson. He's got quite the temper and the person taking care of Josie just can't give the little girl back to him."

Jenna grabbed the phone. "He came here to get her on a motorcycle, and he was drunk and didn't have a helmet for her. Then he called her a 'twat' and threatened to hit me."

"Oh goodness. I'm so sorry ma'm, though he is her legal father. We recommend you get a lawyer and do the work to help Josie so she doesn't go back to him. We'll need the child while things are figured out though. She can be placed with a foster family. She will be safe. We're not sure she can go to you though as you are not her family."

Jenna knew of the news stories of foster families where foster children were abused or lost in the system. She didn't like this idea.

"I'm not sure this is ok." Jenna was unhappy.

"This must be very difficult for you. We are here to help. We want the best for her. We do have to take her from you though, at least for the time being, possibly longer. My apologies."

Josie was in shock. She noted "I'm not going anywhere, you're my real momma." But her eyes seemed glazed. She appeared very tired. She didn't say very much more and looked slightly confused or dazed. Jenna comforted her and let her lay down in the car against her side.

Jenna felt her face redden and her heart drop. She didn't want to give up on Josie. This poor child had been through so much.

Josie trembled as she leaned against her. Was she cold or scared or both?

Lewis frowned at them in a protective way. "We'll try to get this worked out." He noted into the phone, hanging up the phone.

Josie looked sad and frowned as she fell asleep from exhaustion.

Jenna mumbled as she fell into exhaustion, "Don't worry honey, I'll see you soon. I'll always care about you ... "

Ralph and Lewis put Sven in the back of Lewis's cop car, and Lewis and Jenna drove Josie to Child Protective Services. They were quiet and sober and Jenna didn't want to complicate things by crying. Lewis's car was warm and smelled clean like him. There was a warm clean flannel blanket in the back of the car. It smelled unused, new. In fact, she and Josie both fell asleep, shocked and exhausted from all of the evening's events, including the earlier events at Lewis's condominium, and a general lack of time today for Jenna to eat. She remembered she had fed Josie which was good. Lately, she didn't find as much time for her to eat, always taking care of others. She was always feeding other people. She didn't want to give Josie up either. She was so tired from trying to think up ways to keep Josie.

Jenna woke up in the morning to the smell of eggs frying, of toast and bacon. Her hands and knees hurt and she nearly cried out when she lifted herself out of bed. She was dressed in a UGA football t-shirt and boxers. She remembered blurred fatigued moments from the evening before. She was a tired mess and Lewis had offered to help her. She had been too worn down to resist so she had agreed, but now she worried she had made the wrong decisions. At first she wondered who had dressed her. "Oh dear, what have I done?"

"Hi." Lewis was in the doorway with a tray. "You want some eggs?"

Jenna crumpled back onto the bed yawning. "I am so tired."

"I would imagine so..."

She was at Lewis's condo. She remembered arriving here, dozing off on his couch. Somehow she had expected to wake up at home. However, she was a little worried about wearing his clothes. She couldn't remember anything more than simply changing into his clothes privately in the bathroom. Jenna smiled as Lewis lowered the tray onto her lap.

"You need some taking care of." He kissed her on the forehead and undid a napkin which he tucked into her shirt. "Now, eat up."

Jenna proceeded to eat the bacon. On television she had heard that Marijuana was a gateway drug for more serious drugs. She considered bacon a gateway food for serious vegetarians. Many friends of hers in high school had called themselves Vegetarians, yet made an exception for well cooked extra crispy bacon. It smelled and tasted so good and salty, and it sang in her tastebuds. Oh how she loved bacon. The eggs went down fast too. She had never had the pizza they had planned on the evening before (she was too amped up because of Lewis) and she was feeling more alive and awake now that she was eating. Lewis lifted the coffee and sat next to her on the bed. He took a sip and ran his hand along her arm.

"Oh shit!" Jenna shot up, almost overturning the tray. She had forgotten about work somehow. Jojo would be real mad. "I didn't show up at work!" Lewis raised his coffee so she didn't hit it in her sudden jump upright in bed.

"Relax. It's all taken care of. Keesha has it under control." His hand stayed on her arm and she relaxed.

She remembered Keesha from that evening, cleaning up glass and giving Josie cookies and milk to go so that Josie had something to eat. She remembered Keesha's hand on her forehead, Keesha hugging her and Keesha's worried look at Lewis.

"There's no emergencies? Where's Josie?"

Lewis laughed and patted her. "She's fine. Sven accosted my buddy, a fellow officer, Joe Blankenship, who had tried to wake him up, so he'll be in jail for a little while longer, and Joe took a statement about how Sven planned to treat the little girl – he was still drunk when he woke up. I don't think he'll be seeing her for a little while. Joe is fine by the way. Has a small bruise on his cheek where Sven grazed him with his fist."

Jenna sighed, relaxing. She sipped the coffee, which was robust and nutty and warmed her up as it went down. "Where is she?"

Lewis left the room.

Instead of Lewis, Josie appeared. "Hi, mama!" Josie came running through the door. Jenna nearly spilled her coffee all over herself. She tickled Josie's side and rolled sideways when Josie gave her a big strong hug. She laughed and then she cried. Words could not express her relief at having Josie with her once again. She thought she had lost her.

"I'm not your real mama dear, but I will always be here for you, I will always be a momma to you." She fed Josie some eggs and bacon.

Josie grabbed a piece of bread off the tray. "You're my mama now. Lewis taught me how to make eggs! I made the eggs for you!"

"Cool. So smart, you're learning things so quick. How you doing, my lovely daughter?"

"Good. Lewis says I can take self-defense lessons, so I can fight like you did with Sven. I plan on keeping all the boys in line. I want to be tough and I want to show Buttercup who's boss." Josie was going a mile a minute, talking like no end was in sight. She was glad that Josie was ok, glad to see her little cherub healthy and cared for. She loved Josie dearly and knew that she would be a part of her life no matter where she ended up.

Buttercup. Jenna wondered how Buttercup was doing.

Lewis appeared in the door with a couple of pieces of paper. "It's just a draft, but I thought I'd help with your legal defense."

"Legal defense?" All that is good never lasts long.

"You are bringing Sven to court to take custody of Josie. And I need you to sign this second restraining order for Josie."

"What about her mom?"

"She disappeared six months ago. She was pretty heavy into drugs, unfortunately. A body was found that matched hers a while back near Sven's home, but has not yet been identified." Jenna looked down. Was Sven capable of killing someone? She thought perhaps so.

"Lewis, you're a godsend."

"You're so beautiful." Lewis's eyes went to her lips. His pen seemed to caress the sides of the pieces of paper. Here we go again, thought Jenna. She knew he would be respectful of Josie though. She felt the familiar stir in her stomach, that yearning for him, but she kept it in check. A child took different rules, and took raising, not as a friend, not as a caregiver, but as a mother. And a [possible future] mother had certain responsibilities. She really wanted to kiss Lewis though.

CHAPTER 8
CHIEF FINDS A VOICE

The power of silence is not lost on a wise soul.
– Chief Proverb

They had sold Jenna's trailer and were at Ma's old house, which backed up to a new horse barn on the south side. The Sawyers had wanted a farm, and the land had sold just one month previous to them. So Jenna also had new neighbors. Jenna's mom's house needed a great deal of upkeep. The neighbors had wanted to assume her Ma's house too, and Jenna thought it was in a better neighborhood, which meant better schools, than the trailer was and needed less fixing up. It's sad that the communities with less money, get a worse education. Unfortunately, in America, sometimes money does help you get along in life; quite literally. The house was a washed out red with what was once white trim, now gray with dirt. The backyard was overgrown with blackberries and kudzu, and a half rotten apple tree that needed to be removed, roots and all. In the front, the sidewalk buckled under the weight of a 200 year old oak tree that towered above both house and road. The house would take time and fixing up, but it was a keeper. There were a few kids that lived on the road and they liked to play games with Josie.

Josie was into fort building, soccer, and Barbie dolls. She would build forts with her friends in the woods, and then play Barbie in the evening just before her favorite cartoons started on television.

Jenna's ma had only left them the house. With the money she had received for her small patch of land and her trailer and her ma's old trailer sale in savings for Josie, she had decided to set up another savings fund for Josie's college years, and she had given Chief a small amount of money to start his own horse training business. The Chief had decided to save and wait, building up a client list. He just really seemed content keeping busy.

This house brought back memories. Why Ma didn't live here or have her come here in the first place was a mystery. It was definitely in worse shape than the trailer in some respects. However, it was safer with much more potential and in a better neighborhood. Her Ma's house needed fixing up. And it was a historic house – having been a farmhouse and then a schoolhouse in the 1800s. There was a rusty old plaque that Jenna remembered from the basement. "Built in 1892" it said in large black serifed Roman letters carved in metal. The porch in front of the house was leaning sideways, but the Chief had noted that it was safe to stand on, just needed some new boards in the right places.

"Your Ma wouldn't let me do much work on the house. She was scared I would judge her or think poorly of her for not taking good care of it.."

Interesting. Her Ma should have let Chief do some work. Vera had always been stubborn. She never did have good taste in men until the Chief. She remembered her mother and a boyfriend fighting. The hallway wall still had the dent in it where her mother's drunk boyfriend had punched the wall in frustration. Jenna remembered how scared she was, how Vera had locked her in the basement to keep her safe. Jenna was a little clostrophobic because of it. Basements full of dust and rusty moving sweating pipes had always scared her since spending too much time in one. Yes, they would have to fix up and clean out that basement.

The house had been in her family for some time. She wondered how Claudette had not swooped into town yet after her mother's death. Perhaps she still didn't know.

Jenna also remembered the time she and her mother had painted the kitchen walls. Jenna had wanted green walls, but Vera wouldn't have it. "I want some nice clean white walls for once" Vera had mumbled. The walls were a dark yellow with dirt and grime, the soot of Vera's many smoked cigarettes. Now, the kitchen walls were white with a hint of yellow to them. Jenna smiled, sometimes the grime of life still shows. She'd put another coat of white on the kitchen walls. For once, she agreed with her dead mother. It'd be nice to have clean white walls.

"I have a new lady in my life."

Though daydreaming about her past, Jenna came to, staring at the Chief in disbelief. It's just too early.

Chief chuckled and he paused, laughlines danced along this eyes and mouth creasing. "A cute little palomino. I'm training her – she's my newest client. Er, well, her owner is my newest client, but she is who I'm training."

"How cool, Chief, congrats." Jenna held a mug of warm dark chocolate cocoa in her hands. She sipped it and relaxed.

Later on, the vet came to get Josie to go and visit Butterball.

The vet was going to bring Josie to the vet school, and the Chief insisted on going too. He had become protective of her and didn't want her going alone with someone they did not know too well.

Josie came back very happy. Betty/Butterball had survived, Josie yelled, and the baby had not been too too big, but big enough for the necessity of surgery unfortunately, though. The pony had a little bit of a fever, but she was better. The baby was healthy and definitely a little attention monger just like mom. Josie kept talking and talking about her pony and she had even named the foal. She wanted to call it Hammy. The Chief disagreed. "It's best to wait, she'll tell you her name with time."

"But she already told me her name." Josie stammered, dark curls bounced and emphasized her point.

"Hammy?" Jenna asked theatrically. Who names a horse that?

"Putting an ad in Stablemates for horse training." Chief stated at dinner. Josie had been sad that they didn't like the name Hammy. She had walked with Chief while he put up electric fencing for Buttercup on the property next door. It was nice to not be borrowing pasture from a neighbor. This was her home.

Josie was concerned an electric fence might hurt Betty and Hammy. "I don't understand why he can't have a big fence, like before?"

"Cause he's crafty, like a mouse." The Chief stated. "An electric fence will also keep G from causing us more problems. If he comes here for Betty, we can build a fence like this for him too." Josie seemed to then understand why he was doing what he was doing.

Jenna was now feeling as if a healthy family life was starting on the new old farm. Chief brought a stability and calmness to their lives and Josie brought joy and laughter. It occurred to Jenna that it took her mother's death for her to open up to his new life with Chief, Josie, Lewis, Keesha and her new job. This saddened her because she loved her mother dearly. Her mother's passing had taught her many things about not giving up. You never know what possibilities exist in life.

The Chief was now working at the barn next door to the property, and often slept there. He came to get Josie for lessons and for her weekly cleanup. Jenna had decided that Josie would need to work to earn Buttercup's keep at the barn.

Geez that was a fat pony. Buttercup remained fat after the pregnancy. They tried every diet they could. They read an ad in the paper about Meadowbrook farms – the place where Butterball came from. It said that she had over twenty years experience. Michelle had seemed about twenty years old. How do you have experience when you are a year old? Ah well, were Horse It Alls – 'prone to exaggeration?', she asked Chief. Yes, he had said with emphasis. He invited her on his walk with Josie and Buttercup. She was amazed about all the things he had to say. She had never heard him talk so much. She wanted to ask him why he chose to talk on the walks. She imagined he would tell her that there is a time to talk and a time for silence. She loved his quotable sayings.

Josie's question that evening was – "Chief, do you think that your horse business will do well?"

"Well of spirit, or well of money?"

"Both?" Josie turned her nose up.

"It is important to be well of spirit, because money doesn't matter. Actually, I would say that well of spirit, attracts you the money because then it finds you instead. I find some peace in calming horses – I feel like it is a calling – like the mouse realizes he wants to help the lion. I have found that this helping animals helps me to find a peace – helps me find a peace. I don't care for too much money either. I think that endeavors that involve the sole seeking of income, bring only money without spirit and I think that the money without spirit or goodwill will fall through your fingers like sand, it is meaningless, it dangerous. It was not earned for good. It was earned only to earn it. Such income prospects can never last."

"Ok." This seemed a little above Josie's head. But Josie took it in and had a very serious look on her face. "I love Buttercup."

"Yes, Buttercup likes you too. He often changed his grazing habits for when you came home. Do you know, he settles for the shorter grasses, when he knows you'll be home soon, so he can watch your arrival."

"Really? Buttercup makes me well of spirit."

"He *helps* you be well of spirit. Have I told you the story of the Lion and the mouse?" Chief asked us.

"No." they said in unison. Jenna walked through tall grasses and enjoyed the sun on her shoulders. She wore a tube top and some shorts she had made from an old pair of jeans. She had sowed in the hem at the help of a lady who used to work with her at Super-Mega-Mart who was helping her to learn to sow. She found herself to be quite a multi-tasker. She had also found an old sewing machine in a cabinet in the attic. It looked like an antique. Had her grand Aunt used it?

"Well, there was once a lion, angry mean thing that roamed the jungle and he hated everyone and everything. For a lion he was himself, relatively lost, but himself. Teared up animals on a regular basis, ate what he wanted, cared for nothing and lived a life with no soul, or a general lack of soul. He had not yet found his sense of self. He was an angry lonely lion with no roots.

One day the lion was roaming the forest, when he stepped on a splinter. This mighty beast could bring down a

1600 pound rhino, but with his monstrous claws, he had no means for getting rid of a splinter. He found himself crying. He cried and cried and cried. It hurt more than his play fights. It hurt more than the time he had sprained his paw in a hole he had mistakenly stepped in. It hurt more than the time when the squirrel he had attacked had bitten his foot. It hurt alot.

So, he found himself crippled with a splinter stuck deep in his paw and it was infected and he could not walk on it. His paw was starting to swell. His problem had spiralled out of control. Change was needed.

That day, a small mouse happened upon him. It was a kind mouse with a strong sense of soul. This mouse was on a hitchhike through the jungle to meet the mighty spirit. He liked to visit the mighty spirit, once every five years. He carry a stick with a bag over his shoulder. All his belongings in this bag.

So, the mouse told the lion – 'I will take the splinter out of your paw, but you cannot eat me. I know you must be hungry, but you'll have to prove to me that I can trust you.'

The lion growled and chuckled at the mouse. 'I will not eat you, little one.' But the lion was very hungry and drool hung off his jowls. You see, he hadn't eaten in a couple of days either. His eyes were wild with hunger and desperation.

Luckily, the mouse knew what he saw and he decided it was not the lion's time. Instead they hung out and talked for hours, giving the lion a little water from a nearby stream – the lion was very grumpy about the whole thing, but he complied and soon he started to forget about the pain in his paw. He started to laugh about the mouse's silly jokes, and he liked to hear about the mouse's little brother who the mouse would get in trouble all of the time. And after the lion had forgotten the pain, the mouse pulled the splinter out of the lion's foot. 'Now you are ready to go back and live life.' The mouse told the lion."

"You see, the lion had to have hardship, in order to understand how good his life had been before. To appreciate the little things in life."

Josie giggled. "I am too small to be a lion, but I felt like that lion for a little while."

Jenna thought the story sounded familiar but couldn't exactly place it.

"Hmmm."

And that was the end of the talking for that evening.

"Now we learn the art of silence." The Chief and Josie took in their beautiful surroundings and smelled the fresh air. Grass swayed in the breeze. Bees hummed and flowers rustled.

CHAPTER 9
CHOCOLATES AND PROMISES

Trying loving yourself so you can best love others.
—Chief Proverb

Jenna was hopeful that her legal case for adoption of Josie was going well. She had no idea but she hoped for the best. She knew that she had filed multiple papers and two restraining orders were in place against Sven. He was not allowed near either of them at the very least. Jenna was a registered foster home so that she could care for Josie until things were figured out. At least everything was now legal and Jenna didn't have to worry about that. This made her feel more secure and likely helped Josie feel more secure as well.

Sven had a number of run-ins with the law and felt he couldn't get any justice in that town and felt he was being unfairly singled out when he believed he hadn't done anything wrong. After a while, he decided to get on his motorcycle and ride across country and settle down where "they treated people right." he said he was never coming back to this "shit hole" of a place and for the first time in a long time, Jenna actually thought he might keep that one promise. She sure hoped so. Child Protective Services had given up on Sven and were considering Jenna's application for adoption. In the meantime Josie had settled back into going to school and was making good grades, this time not missing any school. Josie seemed at ease at home and Buttercup and Hammy gave her a lot of joy. Jenna came to love Chief, not in a romantic way of course, but as a father figure that she never had. She was thankful everyday that he had come into her mother's life and now into her life.

Jenna's boss JoJo gave gave her a slight raise for her good performance. Though it wasn't much money, it meant more to Jenna just that she had a thoughtful boss and a good place to work. She had never been given a raise before so this was a cause for celebration. Lewis, Chief, Josie and Jenna went out for dinner to celebrate as a result.

They went to a new restaurant in town, which was already known for having good margaritas. Jenna was always conscious of what she drank and nervously sipped on a diet coke instead of a margarita. She would never end up like her mother. At the same time, she had cause to celebrate. Chief had a water, with lemon, no margarita. Josie had a shirley temple (no alcohol of course). Lewis also had water. They all talked and laughed. Josie sat between Jenna and Chief but she beamed at Lewis and Keesha. Jenna was happy to see Josie happy.

"Jenna, I am so glad to see you happy." Keesha gave her a hug as she sipped her drink, a chocolate martini.

"I don't know how I got where I am, honestly."

"Someone was looking out for you." Keesha nodded at Lewis and at her.

"I had some strength didn't I?" She knew Keesha had nodded at Lewis but she couldn't resist.

"You're smart, you're strong, you're beautiful, my dear."

"So are you Keesha, I am so blessed to have you as my friend. And I'm blessed with you too Lewis." Jenna blushed.

"I'm beautiful?" Lewis was trying to make a joke, but noticing Jenna's blush. "Jenna you're not just beautiful, you're gorgeous and talented too."

Their food arrived and they talked over warm food. Jenna avoided the chips as they were fried and she was avoiding fried foods. Given that Josie was growing, she allowed Josie to eat chips when eating out. This was also a celebration so she didn't limit Josie to healthful foods at the restaurant this time though at home they had 1-2 servings of vegetables with lunch and dinner meals. Honestly though, Josie mostly ate healthfully without prodding. Josie had ordered spinach enchiladas with half cheese and a salad instead of rice and beans which was uncharacteristic of most children, noted Keesha.

"You're going to have to come over and eat green things in front of Zeena. Tell her just how good they taste." Noted Keesha to Josie. Keesha loved veggies. She was currently reading a book called "How Not to Die" focused on how eating healthy foods can save your life.

Jenna could see that Lewis was staring at her with some intensity. What was he up to?

The next day, Jenna arrived early to work after driving Josie to school. Josie was excited about her history project. She had created a map showing two battle sites of the revolutionary war. Chief had helped her with it.

Jenna found she had a great deal more energy lately. She had cleaned out the old Chevy and bought a used mechanic's manual for her model Chevy to try to figure out how to do her oil changes herself. Driving a cleaner, more manageable car to work simplified her life. She had thought about getting a newer car, but a free car versus car payments made absolutely no sense. She needed to save money, not spend it. She was fortunate that the community college held semi-annual used book sales. The automotive department on campus had a lot of used mechanic books for sale. She would just fix the old tank herself if need be. Josie had also taken an interest in helping her clean and fix up the car and things around the house. She was such a good kid.

Keesha was behind her desk, arguing with JoJo on the phone. She had a small box of exotic chocolates displayed with a note from her Ralph to share with her friends, and her pink nail polish was next to her monitor. On Keesha's monitor was a smiling picture of Zeena and Ralph In the photo, Zeena beamed up at Ralph. Little ornate hearts that Keesha had graphically added to the photo adorned the monitor. The hearts looked a little bit like Keesha's henna art. A photo of Jenna and Josie at a dinner at Keesha's home taken a week ago was on the other side of her monitor. Jenna remembered Keesha telling her she wanted a photo to have at work. "So I can smile about my friends." Keesha's perfume wafted through the room like some sort of fragrant and delicious air freshener. Keesha had a frown on her normally complacent face. She appeared slightly stressed.

Jenna was working on the department budget. She was wondering how much JoJo wanted to allocate for student projects, for the yearly conference to be held in November and also for a few other smaller items. There was a new sticky on the budget from JoJo. It noted, "look at last year's budget, add 15% if you think it is a good idea." Ok, Jenna went to the files for last year's budget. Was 15% a good idea? She would look at the budget for last year and also what was actually spent. She thought perhaps she could come up with an appropriate mathematical formula that could be used every year if it made sense.

She had agreed to attend a women's leadership symposium with Keesha on Thursday evening and was looking forward to it. Keesha empowered Jenna and had faith in her. She was a strong and dependable friend. They had gone shopping at one time for a gift for Lewis and Ralph at Barnes & Noble and had also gone out for lunch many times as well. Keesha appreciated spicy food just like Jenna did. They both tended to eat healthy too, but had had some funny experiences. They often tried to eat at new establishments or share new recipes at work. Sometimes they picnicked on the community college commons lawn, a garden was next door that was started by the horticulture department. Sometimes fragrant smells came from that wonderful garden. Jenna wondered if Keesha would find a chocolate some day filled with such delicate fragrances.

Since there was a University a few towns over they sometimes had eccentric establishments pop up. A new "Superhealth Greenery" had opened up near campus. It was a health joint with health shakes and veggie appetizer plates. The chef was from Los Angeles and had received funding from a local rock star. It advertised "no fruit, no nuts, no grains, no soy, nothing evil."

Jenna had ordered "pico foam." She wasn't sure what this was. She thought it would be some sort of vegan cheese dip given the picture on the menu. She noticed dehydrated chips with it on the menu and she craved chips though she avoided the fried ones.

The dish that came out made Keesha laugh and they both could not stop laughing for five minutes. They had decided to share it to save money. It appeared to bubble and diminish after it arrived as it contained great amounts of air.

Jenna had received a literal foam made of tomatoes and onions with a hint of cilantro. Next to it were a couple of 2 centimeter long chips made of some sort of vegetable styrofoam. It was absolutely the worst thing she had tasted and it was akin to eating air. Keesha's and her stomach had gurgled in hunger all day that day. The appetizer also cost her $3. It was cheaper due to being a college town, but still a waste of money for her and Keesha. She and Keesha agreed to be more practical and eat at establishments that provided them with appropriate portions since they liked to share food. But Keesha couldn't resist bringing up the topic of "we ate vegetable foam air!" It made Jenna smirk every time. She thought celery had more substance than "pico foam." Many of the college students raved about "Superhealth Greenery." It also made Keesha and Jenna giggle when students talked about how good it was.

Jenna could see Lewis walking through the lobby doors at work, but he did not see her yet. He looked very well groomed. Both his shirt and his pants looked ironed. He had flowers with him. He looked a little nervous. He was not in uniform but she saw his work communications device attached to his hip. She was enjoying staring at him and didn't want to interrupt him. She thought he was likely here to see her, but didn't want to presume anything.

"No, I can't get myself in here on July 1. It's my anniversary. I know we have our yearly conference at that time. I understand it is our most important conference. Jenna will be fine. She gets it, yeah she definitely understands the importance of the conference. You know, I'm starting to see my little duckling take off. She has an eye for organization. Hey, why don't we discuss this in person? Oh." Keesha smiled at her, big gap and beautiful red lips rising on her satin face.

Keesha hung up the phone in exasperation. Apparently JoJo liked to organize the yearly conference at least a few months ahead of time. It was a conference for community colleges in Georgia, usually held in the Hilton in Downtown Atlanta. Very prestigious for JoJo, very important that they appear organized and put together a top-notch demonstration. She let out a sigh and put her nails where she could see them. "Lord, that is a nervous lady. At times, very high-strung but she does have a lot of responsibilities. She is getting nervous about the conference again. We have the yearly conference coming up and Ralph wants me to –" She turned in her chair.

Keesha suddenly noticed Lewis sitting in a chair in front of them. She was spooked by his sudden presence. How had he been so quiet? How had she not noticed him, she wondered?

She jumped in her chair. "Oh dear lord, you nearly gave me a fit. How did you sneak in here?"

"I didn't want to interrupt." Lewis put up his hand and walked up the counter. He looked healthy and beaming, especially when he noticed Jenna. He had a pencil behind his ear.

"I sneaked a peak at your grade, Jenna. A high B, I think you need an A. We need to study more often at my place."

"I think that's actually how I achieved the B in the first place. If I study at your place much more, I'll get a C." Jenna couldn't believe she'd said it. She even felt her lips curl up into a smile. Oh dear. She was joking with him. She was becoming more comfortable with Lewis.

"That's why I'm here Jenna. I wanted to talk to you … in private." He looked as Keesha and smiled sheepishly. "I'm sure Jenna will fill you in on it later."

"That's just mean Lewis, downright mean!" Keesha sashayed out in to the records room, pretending to peek around the door and blowing Jenna a kiss. "You hurt Jenna's heart, I hurt you physically. I am serious. I'll be back soon my best friend." Keesha hugged Jenna as she left the room.

"She seems protective of you." Lewis remarked warily.

Jenna sat down next to Lewis who lifted her chin and looked in her eyes. They hugged, but Lewis was distant and clearly nervous. She tried to kiss him, but he kept her at bay. She liked his smell, Lever2000 and the light musky cologne she noticed from that night... He had on his walkie talkie and she was sure that he had made sure the button was off this time.

He was so nervous. Was he breaking up with her?

"Jenna, well, we have to talk about this."

"Yes."

"I know I'm not real emotional or romantic." Lewis was looking at her eyes.

"You're fine Lewis. You're a good person and that's all that matters." Jenna started to sweat. She tried to smile. "In fact, you're the best person to ever happen to me besides Josie... and of course Keesha."

"I thought about this all day and I cannot wait. I want to do the right thing." He dug down into his pocket and pull out a piece of cloth. The cloth had someone's initials on it. "I had thought about taking you out for a nice dinner or some fanfare but I just am so excited about it, about you. It's an antique."

"Lew, you're making me nervous." Jenna let out a shaky laugh. Antique? Was he giving her furniture?

"Shit, am I doing this all wrong?" He hadn't heard him cuss but once before with her.

"Doing what?" Jenna asked.

Lewis pulled a ring out of the cloth and placed in her left ring finger. It fit well, snug on her finger. She had small fingers. "Jenna, we're old enough that we can know each other a short time and know that, well, we're made for each other…right? Will you marry me?" It was Lewis's grandmother's engagement ring, passed down in Lewis's family. He had inherited it five years ago. His mother had expected him to become engaged some time back, since she desperately wanted grandchildren. She lived in Atlanta, so he didn't see his mother as often as he would like.

Jenna smiled and her stomach did a few leaps of happiness. Oh wow. Oh wow. "Oh wow, Lewis. I'm stunned. Apoplectic."

"I didn't want us to start a relationship without the substance of commitment and well, if you can't keep Josie, I want to help you to see her and I want us to have a child, or whatever you want to do, I just want you around, I want to keep you safe. I want a family with you. We will work hard to give the best life possible to Josie and ourselves and any other children we create."

A cloud of happiness was raining on Jenna and her eyes were misting up. She hugged Lewis. "Oh my goodness, yes! YES! I want a family with you too Lewis." She had hoped Josie wouldn't be an issue for Lewis.

He jumped up and hoisted her up in the air. They kissed deeply, she tugging on his upper lip, snuggling in his neck, smelling his clean Lever2000 smell.

Suddenly Keesha was behind them, hugging them both. It is about time you did that, Lewis. You listened to me. I always know what I am talking about."

"Wait, how –?" Lewis and Jenna both looked at Keesha and burst out laughing. "You couldn't help yourself, could you Keesha?" She guessed that Keesha had been listening in on them.

"It was that or beat him up. I was worried he was going break your heart. He was up to something, being all nervous and everything!" Keesha grinned.

"I was worried Keesha wouldn't let me see you Jenna. I was so nervous. Oh, here are some flowers too for you and Keesha." Lewis passed the flowers to Keesha.

Keesha took the flowers and looked for a vase in the cabinets. "No chocolates?"

"Sorry Keesha, just the antique ring for Jenna." Keesha frowned at him and at Jenna.

"You should stop by with chocolates tomorrow?" Jenna asked slowly, nodding at Keesha. Lewis nodded in agreement.

Lewis's walk-talkie blared with static. "Uh, Lewis, we got a crowd here that's wishin' you the best. However, don't expect us to stop picking on you about this one." Jenna and Lewis heard clapping over the Walkie Talkie in the static and laughs and hoots and hollers. "You better invite us all to your wedding! When's the big day?"

He turned red. "Gosh Darn it!" Lewis took off the Walkie-Talkie, unjamming the snarky button and throwing it across the room. It hit the wall and slid down quickly to the floor in a crash of metal. But it was somehow still on.

"Lewis, Sherriff Johnson is planning you a big celebration party!" More hoots and hollers. The walkie talkie started to fill with static and the whine of a low battery. Finally, thought Jenna. That thing worked too well until now.

But then they both laughed about it and Lewis and Jenna proceeded to kiss. "Don't worry Jenna, I won't let them get too crazy with my party. You can be there too if you want. In fact I would be more comfortable if you were there so they don't get too creative."

Keesha ran to her computer to google "chocolates for a wedding." She had a wedding to plan.

"I'm your Maid of Honor Jenna!" Keesha exclaimed. Jenna wouldn't have it any other way. "I have postcards to design. Oh Jenna I can make you some beautiful henna art! I am taking a website class too, we can even build you a photo website!" Jenna worried about a website but then asked Keesha if the website could be password protected. "Yes, I'll figure it out." Exclaimed Keesha.

"I will be by to pick you and Josie up for dinner if that's ok? Have you heard about the Superhealth Greenery? I don't usually eat that kind of food but it's new and you seem to like vegetables?" Lewis appeared at peace, happy.

Jenna laughed. "I know I eat healthy, but that place is over the top!"

Keesha started to laugh. "We had a bad experience there."

"How about a burger or barbecue?"

"Now you're talking." Jenna knew she could substitute some healthy options with her burger.

Jenna thought about her new life. She had some important revelations. An education really does make a difference in this world as it had helped her immensely. She was now able to live a more comfortable life. She hoped that Josie would continue to get good grades in school so she could make a good life for herself too. Love can be a horrible difficult road, but if you just keep a sense of optimism about your chances for love, your spirit can rise up and meet with another person who feels the same way. Though her trials and tribulations with Sven had been absolutely horrible, she now understand that there were good relationships in this world as well. Jenna felt grateful for her new life. She felt fulfilled and happy and wondered why she hadn't realized her potential previously. Perhaps she'd needed a Sven to know how good life could be with Lewis.

"Lewis, how did I become so lucky to have you in my life." She massaged his shoulders.

"I am the lucky one, Jenna." He beamed at her as she felt the ring on her finger.